Finding Motive
A Rescue Alaska Mystery

by

Kathi Daley

This book is a work of fiction. Names, characters, places, and incidents either are products of the author's imagination or are used fictitiously. Any resemblance to actual events or locales or persons, living or dead, is entirely coincidental.

Copyright © 2022 by Katherine Daley

Version 1.0

All rights reserved, including the right of reproduction in whole or in part in any form.

Chapter 1

The rutted dirt path narrowed as it wove its way across the barren landscape peppered with shrubs that grew along a wide glacier-fed river. It was early summer, creating a cycle of almost never-ending light, which allowed him to make the journey late into the evening. As he approached the small cabin, he began to hum. His appetite for the kill intensified with each nightly visit. He knew that he only had a bit longer to wait until this leg of his journey was complete, and he would be free to move on. He paused at the front door of the cabin. It was small and weathered and hadn't been lived in for at least a decade. He wanted to savor the anticipation that sent his heart racing as he swung the door open and witnessed the look of terror in the man's eyes. Oh, how he loved the sweet taste of the power he knew would only be had once the man surrendered completely. Setting the tray of food and water he carried on a nearby table, he smiled at the man and spoke. "It won't be long now. A few more days and this will all be over." With that, he turned, exited the cabin, locked the door behind him, and retraced his steps back down the same path he'd just traveled.

I woke with a start. My heart pounded as I remembered with absolute clarity the rage and pain the man trapped in the windowless room was feeling. I can't say that I specifically knew what the man might be experiencing, but the look of total surrender in his eyes seemed to tell it all.

I rolled over and turned my bedside light on. My golden retriever, Honey, lifted her head, but when she noticed me opening the drawer of the bedside table, pulling my journal and a pen out, she lowered her head and went back to sleep. I'd been having similar dreams for months, although the physical location, as well as the identity of the captive being held in the locked room, seemed to have changed. I wasn't sure what happened to the hostages once their time was up. I assumed they were killed, allowing the man who'd brought the food the freedom to move on to a new hostage and a change of venue.

This week, the captive in my dreams was the third victim I'd witnessed. The first victim, a woman with red hair, who'd been locked in a warehouse in the middle of what appeared to be a large city, had first shown up in my dreams three months ago. I'd dreamt of the woman three times, observing her through the eyes of the individual with the food. I wasn't sure how much time had actually passed between the three visits, but my sense was that the woman had been held for at least two weeks, perhaps longer.

Eventually, she was replaced by a man who was being held in a shed near a lake. After six visits to the man in the shed in my dreams, which spanned fifteen days in real-time, this hostage had been replaced by the man I'd visited tonight. This was my fifth dream involving this particular captive. I'd first dreamt of him thirteen days ago. Based on the previous pattern, I knew that the man in the locked room would be replaced by someone new within the next few days. The man with the food never seemed to keep those he held for more than three weeks. As far as I could tell, the actual duration of the captivity was closer to two weeks, but since the timelines seemed varied, it was hard to pin down an exact duration.

Tonight's dream felt different, I wrote in my journal. *I was able not only to witness the scene that unfolded through the eyes of the man with the food, but I was also able to feel what he felt as he delivered the food. I feel sure these visitations have been visions rather than dreams. I know in my heart that the man in the room is being held hostage and needs my help, but so far, I've been unable to see anything that will help me to find him.*

I set the journal on my lap and tried to create a clear picture in my mind of everything I'd just witnessed. Back when these strange and disturbing dreams began, I hadn't paid a lot of attention to them, but as time went by, I began to wonder if perhaps the dreams weren't more than dreams. If they were visions, it wouldn't be the first time this sort of thing had happened. I had a unique ability that allowed me to connect mentally with specific individuals, and this past year, that gift seemed to have grown and expanded, allowing me to connect with those individuals during my dream state. After several dreams about the same woman in the locked warehouse three months ago, I decided to fill my friend, Police Chief Hank Houston, in on things. Houston had conducted a missing persons search, but no one fitting the description of the woman in my dreams showed up in either Alaska or the Western United States.

Not long after Houston began looking for the woman in my dreams, she'd been replaced by a man locked in the shed near the lake. If I was experiencing a connection with the man or woman who imprisoned these individuals, he seemed to have moved from one location and one victim to another every few weeks. Based on the landscapes I'd briefly been able to view, I had no idea which city the warehouse had been located in or which lake the shed had been situated near. Based on the landscape from tonight's dream, I was going to go out on a limb and say the man with the food had found his way to Alaska.

Once I'd written down every single detail I could remember, I put the journal back in the drawer, turned the light off, and attempted to go back to sleep. I knew that obsessing over the individuals I dreamed about was only going to make me ill, so I tried to compartmentalize as Houston had suggested. I wanted very much to help those who guest-starred in my dreams, but after months of trying, I really hadn't gotten anywhere. I'd looked at photos until I was cross-eyed from trying to identify the city where the warehouse from the first set of dreams was located but had never been able to narrow it down beyond an industrial area with similar warehouses as far as the eye could see.

The shed on the lake had been even harder to identify. There were just too many lakes in the world to settle on a location. But the landscape in the dreams I'd been most recently having felt familiar. Maybe if I really focused, I'd be able to recognize a landmark and figure out where the man in the cabin was being held.

Honey must have sensed my restlessness since she scooted her way up from the bottom of my bed. She laid her head on the pillow next to me. I found comfort in her warm breath on my face. I loved all my dogs, and each seemed to serve a unique purpose, but Honey was the dog most in tune with my feelings. She was the one who seemed to know when I needed a warm hug and did her doggy best to provide one.

As I drifted off to sleep, I thought about the three victims I'd caught glimpses of so far. I wondered if they were the only three victims of the individual I seemed connected with or if there had been others whose captivity I simply hadn't tuned in to witness. I hoped the victim list had been limited to three, although even three was too many when I saw the terror these individuals were subjected to. I found it sort of odd that Houston hadn't been able to locate any of the victims through missing persons reports. I had been able to come up with fairly good descriptions, although for all I knew, the hostages hadn't even been kept in this country.

I forced my mind to focus on other things as I struggled to return to sleep. It was spring in Alaska, and the disappearance of snow and the arrival of spring flowers accompanied the arrival of long days and short nights. Perhaps I'd take the dogs on a hike up to the meadow. The lake would be lovely at this time of the year. I'd need to watch for hungry grizzlies venturing out from their long slumber. Bears and dogs didn't really mix, so I felt relatively safe when I had my pack of seven to keep me company. Oh, and I needed to call my dear friend, Chloe. She'd left three messages suggesting that I stop by the diner she ran so we could catch up. She'd been hinting around that she had something interesting to share. Chloe and I had known each other for a long time, and I had to admit that I really should take the time to nurture that relationship even if I was busy with aspects of my life that didn't involve her.

Just as I was drifting off, I swore I heard my wolf hybrid, Denali, growl. I supposed it might have been a snort. He did tend to snore at times, and if there was any real danger, he'd be making a lot more racket than a gentle growl. Still, given the fact that the man in my dreams seemed to have found his way to Alaska, I supposed it might behoove me to pay extra attention to my surroundings until I was sure the man with the deep and raspy voice had moved on.

Chapter 2

The following morning, the dogs made it clear that they still wanted their walk even if I hadn't gotten much sleep. I considered a short walk, but then I remembered my idea to head to the lake, so I picked up my cranky cat, Moose, gave him a quick cuddle, and then headed to the bathroom to wash up and dress. Pulling on a dark gray t-shirt, a black zip-up sweatshirt, a pair of old jeans, and my oldest running shoes, I called the dogs, grabbed my rifle, and set off toward the lake. As he always did, my search and rescue dog, Yukon, took a position in the front of the pack with my wolf hybrid, Denali. Shia, an energetic young husky, along with my two retired sled dogs, Juno and Kodi, settled into the middle of the pack while I slowly walked behind so my three-legged dog, Lucky, could keep up. I supposed Honey could have hung with the dogs in the middle of the pack, but she preferred to walk right next to Lucky and me, which is where she tended to settle in once she'd expended a bit of energy.

As I knew it would be, the walk up to the lake was gorgeous. Wildflowers in every color of the rainbow had begun to paint the landscape. The winters in my area were long, and the snow got so deep that there were times I'd wonder if we'd ever see the ground again, but then the long days of spring and early summer would come along and turn the landscape into a magical fairyland.

Once we reached the lake, I turned around, calling the dogs in front of me to return to my side. There were times I'd let the dogs swim for a while before heading back to my cabin, but I actually had a lot to get done before I was supposed to show up for my volunteer shift at the Rescue Animal Shelter.

After we returned to the cabin, I gave the dogs food and freshened their water, cleaned Moose's cat box, refilled his dishes, and then headed out to the barn. I'd just fed the rabbits and was starting to clean the stall of my blind mule, Homer, when the cell phone in my pocket rang. I pulled my phone out and looked at the caller ID. It was Serena Walters, the one and only full-time employee of the shelter I'd founded, my good friend and action superstar, Harley Medford, had paid for, and Serena and her volunteers ran.

I answered, and she responded. "Hey, Harm. I know you hadn't planned to come in until later, but Ed is supposed to cover the desk today while I teach a training class, but he hasn't shown up. I have nine dogs and owners scheduled to arrive in less than an hour, and I'd hate to cancel the class. I hoped you could come in early.

I looked down at my filthy clothes and agreed to come in as soon as I could shower and change. After showering, I decided to let my long curly hair dry naturally rather than taking the time to dry and style it. I grabbed my purse and headed out the door. The class Serena was planning to teach had just started when I arrived, so I poked my head in the door of the training room to let the hardworking woman know I was there, and then I headed to the front desk to speak to the man who'd brought in a litter of puppies to drop off. By the time I'd settled the pups, following my lecture about the importance of spaying and neutering dogs and cats, the contractors who were working on the addition of a wild animal wing to our existing structure had arrived. I'd just gotten them settled when the man who'd paid for the whole thing walked in through the front door.

"Harley!" I screeched as he sauntered into the main lobby of the animal shelter. "I wasn't expecting you until next week."

He smiled. "And here I thought you wore that sunny yellow sweater just for me."

I hugged the man who meant so much to me. "Sorry. I really had no idea you'd be home today, but I'm glad that you are, and I'm glad I just happened to be wearing my new sweater. Did your movie wrap early?"

Harley nodded. "It did wrap early, and I couldn't wait to get home." He turned and held his arm out toward a tall, dark-haired woman who entered the room, walked up, and then stood next to him.

"Harmony Carson," Harley began. "I'd like to introduce you to Brittany Hartland. Brittany worked on the movie I just wrapped, and when she mentioned that she'd always wanted to visit Alaska, I invited her to come home with me and check the place out."

Interesting. "I'm happy to meet you," I said. "Are you an actress?"

"Writer. I worked as part of the team that adapted the novel into a screenplay."

I had to admit that surprised me, although I wasn't sure why I'd just assumed that someone who looked like Brittany would be in front of the camera. "Wow. That's awesome. I hope you enjoy your time in Alaska."

She grinned. Brittney's smile seemed genuine and not contrived, which made me like her more than I thought I would. "I'm really excited to be here. It's always been one of my dreams to come to Alaska, and Harley has been so sweet letting me stay in one of his guest rooms. I can't wait to have a chance to really look around."

"Rescue is a small town, so there isn't a lot to see, but if you like hiking, this is the place to be." I turned toward Harley. "I have a shift at Neverland tonight. The two of you should come by. I can introduce Brittany to the gang."

Brittany raised a brow. "Neverland?"

"It's a bar that also serves as a local eatery," I explained. "I work at Neverland part-time. The food is excellent, and the locals all hang out there, so it's a good place to go to meet everyone."

She looked at Harley. "What do you think?"

He shrugged. "Sounds good to me. I've been missing Sarge's home cooking."

"I work between five and ten tonight, so come by any time between those hours, and I'll make sure you get a good table overlooking the lake."

Harley agreed to my idea and then asked about the expansion we were in the middle of.

"The wild animal cages are coming along just fine. The contractor you hired seems to know what he's doing, and so far, he's sent at least three men to work on our project every weekday, although the same men don't always show up. If you want to see how everything is going, we can walk back there."

"I'd like that," Harley said.

Harley followed me, and Brittany followed him as we walked through the main lobby into a hallway that joined the domestic animal side of the shelter and the wild animal rehabilitation facility we were adding to the property.

"Harley Medford, this is Steve Pierson, Doug Tanner, and Victor Bell. The team from Summit Contracting has made real progress."

"I can see that," Harley said, holding out his hand and greeting each man.

"Mickey said to do a good job for you, so we're giving it our all," Steve said.

Mickey Greenbelt was the owner of Summit Contracting and the man Harley had spoken to before leaving Alaska to film his most recent movie.

"Are we still on track to have the cages and enclosures ready by the first snow?" Harley asked.

Steve nodded. "It's barely June, and we have a good start. I see no reason why we won't be finished by mid-September. Maybe sooner."

"That's wonderful," Harley said.

Brittany hadn't said a word, but I could see that all three men were having a hard time not staring at the strikingly beautiful woman.

"We should go if we're going to be on time to pick the car up that you rented for me," Brittany said to Harley after he'd settled into a conversation with the three men from Summit about the movie he'd just wrapped up.

He glanced at his watch. "Yeah, I guess we should go." He looked at me. "Is Serena around?"

"She's doing a training class," I answered. "I'm sure she won't mind if you stick your head in and say hi."

"I think I'll do that."

I followed Harley as he made his way back to the training room, which was located on the domestic animal side of the shelter. Serena was just wrapping up a class with five women, four men, and nine dogs when Harley and I walked in. She screeched in greeting and then hurried across the room to hug our benefactor much the way I had when I'd first seen him.

"You're back early," she said.

"I am."

"Where's Brando?" Brando was Harley's dog.

"He's at home. Brittany and I have some errands to take care of in town, so I left him to nap."

"Brittany?" Serena asked.

Harley stepped aside and then waved his out-of-town guest over. "Serena, this is Brittany."

Serena's smile faded a bit. "I'm happy to meet you."

I felt so bad for Serena since I knew she had it bad for Harley, which was tough because I was pretty sure that Harley wasn't the settling down sort. I also knew that settling down was something Serena was most definitely interested in.

"So, do you run this place?" Brittany asked.

Serena nodded. "With the help of Harley, Harmony, and a dozen volunteers. Are you visiting our area?"

"Brittany worked on the movie I just wrapped," Harley answered in Brittany's stead. "When I mentioned that I had a home in Alaska, she mentioned that she'd always wanted to visit Alaska, so I invited her to come and stay with me for a bit."

"Wow. That's really wonderful," Serena said through a smile that I was sure was forced. "So, so wonderful," she unnecessarily added. "And how long are you staying?"

Brittany smiled at Harley. "I'm not sure. I guess we'll just see how things go."

"Harley and Brittany were just leaving, so I'll walk them out and then come back to check on your class," I said, giving Serena a way out of this conversation before she broke into tears.

Serena smiled at me. "Thanks. I guess I should get back." She turned to Brittany. "It was good to meet you." She then looked directly at Harley. "Maybe I'll call you later. I have a few things I'd like to discuss with you."

"We're going to dinner at Neverland if you want to come with us," Harley said.

Serena glanced at me. I offered her a glance of support. "No," she said. "I have a lot of paperwork to get through, so I think I'll just stay late and work on that. But maybe you could call me when you get home, and I'll catch you up."

"Okay," Harley said, grabbing Brittany by the hand. "I'll call you after dinner."

Once Harley and Brittany left, I headed to the office Serena and I shared. I didn't have a lot of time to spend at the shelter today since I had a shift at Neverland and needed to get home to get cleaned up before I headed back into town, but since I liked to have a presence, I tried to show up for at least a few hours most days of the week.

"So, what do you make of Brittany?" Serena asked me half an hour later after she'd joined me in the office following her training class.

"I'm not sure," I honestly answered. "The woman is gorgeous and probably just the sort of woman a high-profile action star would date, but Harley made the whole thing sound very casual. I didn't pick up on intimacy of any sort when we were talking earlier. I really just met the woman and can't say for sure, but I won't be surprised if it turns out the two are just friends."

"He invited the woman to come home with him," Serena pointed out.

"He did, but Harley is a nice guy. I can totally see him inviting the woman to Alaska for a visit once he found out that she really wanted to see this part of the country even if intimacy wasn't involved. And he's had other beautiful women stay with him in the past. This certainly isn't the first time he brought someone from his Hollywood life into his Alaska life."

Serena sat down on the chair across the desk from where I was sitting. "Yeah, I guess. Even if this woman is more of a girlfriend than a friend-friend, I'm not in a position to have a problem with it. Harley and I are just friends, the same way you and Harley are just friends. I guess he has a right to date whomever he chooses."

"He does," I agreed. "And, as we've discussed in the past, Harley isn't a full-time resident of Alaska. I know you really like him, but unless you're willing to spend half your time in LA, I really think any sort of relationship you might think you want to have with him beyond simple friendship will likely just lead to heartbreak."

She blew out a breath. "I know, and I've been thinking about that. A lot, actually. The truth of the matter is that for a guy like Harley, I might actually be willing to do the nomad thing."

I supposed if Serena was being honest with herself about that, a relationship with Harley could work, but not only did he have homes in both Alaska and LA, but he traveled all over the world when filming. Serena seemed to be more of a homebody. She loved the animals she worked with and the friends she'd made since moving to Rescue. I honestly didn't think that she'd be as happy living Harley's lifestyle as she thought she might be. At least not in the long run.

"I need to get home," I said. "I have a shift at Neverland later, and I still need to finish cleaning the barn and then clean myself up. I plan to be in tomorrow. Probably around eight. If that changes, I'll let you know; otherwise, I'll see you then."

As I made my way through town toward the remote little cabin where I lived, I thought about the complicated lives many of my friends seemed to live. Life in Alaska wasn't easy. It demanded a lot of you, and the reality was that it was rare for most who came from out of the area to stay. Those who did stay seemed to be in it for life. I know that for me, it was Harley's nomadic lifestyle that helped me to decide not to pursue something romantic with the gorgeous action star. It hadn't been an easy decision since Harley and I had a history, and I actually did think we'd be good together in every other way, but Rescue was my home. It was where I wanted to be. Maybe Serena would be happy gallivanting around the world with Harley, but deep inside, I sort of doubted that to be the case.

After I arrived home, I changed out of my pretty yellow sweater, took the dogs for a quick run, and then began cleaning the barn where I'd left off after Serena had called this morning. Keeping up with the feeding and cleanup of so many animals was almost a full-time job in and of itself, but before the shelter I'd always dreamed of had become a reality, I personally adopted as many strays as needed adopting in order to ensure that all the animals that came into my orbit had a safe and loving place to live. In addition to Homer and the rabbits, who had settled in for the long haul, my barn had previously been home to a baby moose, a bear cub, coyote pups, and even a pair of lynx. Actually, the old barn had been home to the wild animals I now hoped to house in the new wing of the shelter. The barn currently on my property had been built from the ground up after the old barn was destroyed in a fire.

I'd just finished in the barn and was headed back to the house when my cell phone rang. This time it was Houston.

"Hey, Houston," I answered.

"I need your help." He seemed to get right to the point.

"Oh? What's up?"

"I have a missing woman. At this point, I have every reason to believe she's been kidnapped. I'm hoping that you might be able to connect with her. I really have no idea what happened to this young mother, and any help you can give me will be greatly appreciated."

"I'm happy to help," I said. "Where are you?"

"The market in town."

"Okay. I just finished cleaning the barn, so I'll need to change, but I'll be there in a few minutes."

I quickly headed back to the cabin. I washed my hands, pulled on some clean jeans and a clean sweatshirt, then I called my search and rescue dog, Yukon, to come with me in the event the kidnapping turned into a search of some sort. As I drove toward town, I called my brother-in-law, Jake Cartwright, the owner of Neverland, to let him know I'd likely be late to work if I showed up at all. I filled Jake in on the situation and suggested he alert the search and rescue team and have them on standby since they might be needed, depending on how things worked out.

When I arrived at the market the woman had gone missing from, I found Houston, along with his two deputies and a young man holding a toddler, standing near a white sedan.

"So, what's the situation?" I asked.

Houston began to explain. "Rose Bidwell got off work about an hour ago. She picked her two-year-old son, Hunter, up at the daycare center. A clerk remembers Rose coming in with Hunter and buying five or six items. It seems that Rose put the groceries in the back seat then strapped in her son. No one knows what happened next. Another shopper heard Hunter crying approximately fifteen minutes after Rose checked out. She decided to check it out and found Hunter alone in the car. Rose was nowhere to be found."

"So someone likely grabbed Rose after she strapped the toddler into the car but before she was able to walk around the car and get in."

"That's the way it appears," Houston said. "We've looked around the area but didn't find anything that would indicate what happened to the woman. We've also been unable to find anyone who remembers seeing anything."

I looked toward the man holding the toddler. "I take it that's Rose's husband."

Houston nodded. "Jeff Bidwell. He arrived home just a few minutes before we called him asking about his wife."

The man looked to be in shock, which given the situation, I understood.

"I hoped that if you were able to connect with Rose, you might be able to give us a starting point," Houston continued. "To be honest, at this point, all I can assume is that she was pulled into a vehicle and is long gone."

I glanced at the man with the toddler one more time. "I can try. I can't promise anything, but if she's still alive, then maybe. Do you have a photo of the woman? A visual will help."

Houston handed me a photo of a dark-haired woman with long curly hair much like mine. She looked to be about my age and build, and to be honest, I found the similarity somewhat haunting.

I decided to sit in my Jeep while I tried to connect. I needed a quiet place to work without a lot of distractions. Houston knew the drill and slid into the Jeep next to me. I focused on the photo, closed my eyes, and waited for a vision to appear. I'd first discovered that I could connect psychically with those I was meant to save while trying to save my sister, who was lost in a snowstorm when I was seventeen. I'd been unsuccessful on that day, and my sister had died, but my gift had been kindled, and I'd saved quite a few people since then.

"Okay, I think I have her," I said. "She's walking along a river. The trail is narrow and muddy, making it difficult for her to navigate."

"Is she alone?" Houston asked.

"No. There's someone walking behind the woman, but I can't see who it is. The woman is scared and very aware of the presence behind her."

"Can you make out any landmarks?" Houston asked. "We need to figure out where to search."

I tightened my eyes and deepened my focus. Connecting with others always caused horrendous headaches, as well as heightened senses, a state I was just now learning to control. "There's a lake." I paused. "The woman has stopped walking. She still hasn't turned around, but her heart rate is off the charts. I think whatever is going to happen is going to happen here in this spot."

"Which lake, Harm?"

I tried to find a landmark, but since my line of vision was through the eyes of the victim, I could only see what she could see. Eventually, I had it. "Granite Lake. They're at Granite Lake."

Houston jumped into action. He instructed Yukon and me to climb into his four-wheel-drive truck, where his search and rescue dog, Kojak, was waiting for us. Houston then instructed his two deputies to follow in the SUV they'd arrived in. He instructed the man with the toddler to go home and wait for a call. The woman's husband seemed reluctant to leave at first, but Houston could be very forceful when he needed to be, and eventually, the man strapped the toddler into his car and took off down the highway. I called Jake and suggested that he meet us at the trailhead. His search and rescue dog, Sitka, was more experienced than either my dog, Yukon, or Houston's dog, Kojak, were and would come in handy should a search be required. Jake assured me that he'd head to the trailhead with Sitka and a fellow search and rescue team member, Jordan Fairchild. Not only was Jordan a member of the team and Jake's girlfriend, but she was a doctor as well. I informed Houston that Jake was on his way. He was actually starting out closer to our destination, so it was likely he'd beat us there.

Once we'd all arrived at the trailhead, we headed toward the lake. The lake itself was about two miles from the trailhead, but we were motivated to get there quickly, so it took less than half an hour. As we approached the body of water, I began looking for a sign that the woman and her kidnapper were still in the area. I didn't see anyone, but we'd been feeding the scent of a sweater we'd grabbed from the woman's car to the dogs, who had picked the trail up right away. I wasn't sure where the woman was now, but I felt confident that she'd come this way.

Once we reached the lake, the dogs headed around the shoreline in a clockwise direction. Things slowed a bit as it appeared that the woman and her captor might have walked in the water for at least part of the time. It was almost an hour since we'd left the trailhead when I heard the chopper overhead. I looked up to see that search and rescue team member, Dani Mathews, had brought her bird to help in the search.

"Dani to Jake," she said over the walkie-talkie.

"Go for Jake," he responded.

"I have Wyatt with me. He has the glasses, and he said he sees what looks to be someone wearing a red jacket crouched down in the underbrush on the north side of the lake."

"We'll check it out," Jake said. "Do you see only the one figure?"

"Ten-four. I'll take another look and let you know if I can identify a second individual."

By the time we made it all the way around to the northernmost end of the lake, ninety minutes had passed since we'd met at the trailhead. Dani found a meadow to land in, and she and Wyatt were making their way toward us on foot when Houston, Jake, Jordan, and I arrived with the three dogs.

"I think that's Rose," I said, once I got close enough to see the woman sitting on the ground surrounded by the search and rescue dogs who'd run ahead. I picked up my pace, hoping I wouldn't be too late. Jake arrived at the woman sitting on the ground first, followed by Houston, Houston's men, and then me. Jordan arrived just as Dani and Wyatt made their way to the location from the meadow where they'd left the bird.

"I'm Police Chief Hank Houston," Houston said. "Are you Rose Bidwell?"

"I am." The woman sobbed. "My baby. How is my baby?"

"Your little boy is fine. He's with your husband," Houston said as Jake untied the ropes around her wrists and ankles.

The woman looked at me. "Are you Harmony?"

I nodded, "I am."

"I have a message for you."

I raised a brow. "For me?"

She took a shuddering breath. "The man who took me from the market and then dragged me out here said that you'd be coming for me and that when you arrived, I was to tell you the following." She took another deep breath. "He said to tell you that he really liked the yellow sweater you wore today, and he hoped you'd add more color to your otherwise drab wardrobe."

"Yellow sweater?" Wyatt asked. "You have a gray sweatshirt on."

"I was wearing a yellow sweater this morning. Go on. What else did the man say?"

"He said that you can find some of the answers you're seeking at this location." She pulled her red jacket off to reveal a set of coordinates that had been written in ink on her arm. "He also said that he has enjoyed spending time with you and looks forward to the time you will spend with him this evening."

I gasped. "The man who took you must be the same man I've been connecting with during my sleep for the past three months." I looked at the woman. "What did he look like?"

"He had a ski mask on, so I couldn't see his face or hair. His eyes were dark. Brown, I think. He was wearing blue jeans, a blue denim jacket over a white t-shirt, and work boots. Brown."

"How tall was he?" Houston asked.

She shrugged. "I don't know. I guess around six feet. The man didn't seem particularly tall or short, but I can't say with any degree of certainty how tall he actually was."

"How about his voice?" I asked. "Was it deep? High? Did he have an accent?"

She paused and then answered. "Deep. Sort of raspy. Almost as if he had a cold. No accent that I noticed."

That was exactly the voice I remembered hearing during my dreams. If I had to guess, I'd say either the man was a heavy smoker, or he'd had a throat injury at some point.

"Did the guy say anything about the captive he has at the isolated cabin?" I asked as Jake helped the woman to her feet while Jordan made sure she wasn't injured.

"He didn't say anything about a captive. Do you think he has someone else?"

I answered that I had reason to believe that he might.

Jordan asked the woman if she felt okay now that she was on her feet. She wanted to know if she felt lightheaded or dizzy. The woman assured us that she was fine but that her ordeal had been taxing, and she really just wanted to go home. Dani offered to take her in the chopper, but Houston wasn't done with his interview. Once the woman assured him that she'd told me everything she'd been instructed to, Dani took Rose, Jordan, and Houston back to town in the chopper, while Jake, Wyatt, Houston's men, the dogs, and I hiked back to the trailhead where we'd left the vehicles.

"That was weird about the sweater," Jake said as we made the hike back.

"I wore a yellow sweater this morning, so the man must have been stalking me. Or perhaps stalking is too strong a word. Maybe he simply ran into me at some point and noticed the sweater."

"Where did you go when you were wearing the sweater?"

"Just the shelter." I thought back to everyone who'd been at the shelter that morning, but no one stood out as being the likely kidnapper. The idea that someone who was at the shelter might actually be the man I'd been dreaming about for three months sent a chill down my spine.

"What was that part about seeing you tonight?" Wyatt asked.

I'd shared my dreams with Houston and Jake but no one else, so I began to explain. "About three months ago, I had a series of dreams about someone, a male, I think, who had been holding a woman captive in a warehouse. I visited this scene in my dreams three times before I thought it might be more than a dream. As you know, I've experienced connections in my dream state a few times in the recent past, and after three nights of having the exact same dream, I began to suspect that was what was going on. I told Houston what I'd seen, and he asked me to describe the woman who was being held captive. He was never able to find a match in missing persons reports."

"And the kidnapper?" Wyatt asked.

"I witnessed the scene through his eyes, so I never saw his face. I still haven't. I have heard his voice a few times. Deep and raspy." I realized that no one I'd spoken to at the shelter that morning had a deep and raspy voice, so the man who kidnapped Rose couldn't have been anyone I'd talked to. Maybe someone from the dog training class? There were four men, and I only recognized two of them. I'd have to call and ask Serena once we got close enough to town to have cell service.

"And three months later, you're still having this dream?" Wyatt asked.

I nodded. "Things have changed. After a couple weeks, the captive of the man I've been connecting with changed. Victim number one was a woman, and victim number two was a man. The location where the captive was being held changed as well. The first victim, the woman I witnessed as a captive, was held in a warehouse, but the second victim, the man I spent time with, had been held in a shed near a lake. Most recently, I've noticed that the captive is another man. A different man. He seems to be locked in a cabin located in an isolated area."

"Do you think you'll find the cabin at the location corresponding to the GPS coordinates the kidnapper wrote on Rose's arm?"

"I'm not sure, but I certainly hope so." My sense was that the first two victims I'd noticed in the warehouse and the shed were probably dead. I remembered the man in my dreams telling his captives that it wouldn't be much longer. I just hoped that we'd be able to find the captive in the cabin before it was too late.

Houston called me just as we'd returned to the vehicles. He told me that he was at the airstrip and that Jordan had taken Rose to the hospital to be checked out. He asked me to pick him up, after which time he assured me that we'd go in search of whatever we might find at the coordinates our kidnapper had left for me.

Chapter 3

I met Houston at the airfield as instructed. Kojak and Yukon were with me, but Jake had taken Sitka back to the bar. Wyatt had gone with him. Houston's men had gone back to the station where they assured Houston they'd await further instructions.

"While I was waiting for you, I used my cell phone to find the location of the GPS coordinates left for you," Houston informed me.

"And where do they lead?"

"About here." He pointed to a location on a map near the Canadian border.

"That's a pretty long drive from here," I said.

"It is, which is why I asked Dani to take us in the bird. She's refueling and will be by to pick us up in really notice them, but I can say there were a bunch of cars in the lot."

"So someone could have been sitting in one of the cars when you arrived," Houston pointed out.

"Sure. I guess so."

Jake frowned. "I'm not liking this one bit."

Houston's scowl was almost as telling when he agreed that the situation relating to my dreams seemed to have taken a disturbing turn.

"This man seems to know that you've been spending time in his head," Houston said. "Has that ever happened before?"

I paused briefly before answering. "I think that when I make a connection, the person I'm connecting with is aware that someone is there. If the person I'm connecting with during a rescue is lost or injured, I introduce myself and try to calm them until help can arrive. Some rescue victims acknowledge me, while others don't. But connecting during my sleep is something really different. I didn't even know at first that I was connecting. For quite a while, I thought I was just dreaming. By the time I figured out what was actually going on, I realized that the man I was connecting with was the bad guy and not the victim. I've been careful not to reveal myself. At least, I thought I had been careful. Apparently, this guy not only knows I've been in his head, but he knows who I am as well. I've always been in control in the past, but this time feels different. Really different," I emphasized.

Houston, Jake, and I continued to discuss the situation as Dani flew us east. I had a bad feeling about things, and I think the others did, as well. By the time we finally arrived in the remote area of Alaska the coordinates took us to, it was late in the evening. We decided to fly overhead and see if we could spot the cabin from the air. The quickest and probably safest way to get the information we were after was to try to locate the cabin and then land in the same vicinity.

"There," I said, pointing to the ground during our third pass. "I think the cabin is there. Next to the river. I remember there being a river in my dreams, and I remember the path being wet."

"I don't see a cabin," Jake said.

"I bet it's tucked away near that grove of trees growing along the lake to the west. There's a large meadow to the north of the trees. Let's land there and continue on foot."

Everyone agreed to my plan for Dani to set the bird down. Once we'd landed, there was some discussion as to whether anyone should stay with the chopper. Houston didn't want to leave anyone alone, so in the end, it was decided that Dani and Jake would stay with the chopper while Houston and I checked out the situation with the cabin.

"This looks familiar," I said as we walked along the river. "I think we're close."

"I just hope this isn't a trap," Houston said. "Perhaps we should have some backup."

"There wasn't room in the chopper for backup," I insisted. "I really have no idea where this will lead, but I do sense that our finding whatever there is to find before anyone else stumbles across it will be imperative to the answers we're after."

After another forty minutes of walking, the cabin came into view. It didn't look occupied, but there was no telling what we'd find once we entered the structure, so Houston and I both drew our guns and slowly continued forward. My heart began to race as we approached the front door. I remembered that the kidnapper's heart began to race as he approached this same door during my dream last night.

The first thing I noticed after we opened the door was that with the exception of a single table and a man lying face down on the floor, the cabin was completely empty. Houston slowly approached, his gun still drawn. He bent down to check the man's pulse, but he was gone. Based on the condition of the body, I sensed that he'd probably died shortly after my dream the previous evening.

"Something happened to make this man change his timeline," I said.

"Why do you say that?" Houston asked.

"The man I've been channeling kept the other victims for between two and three weeks before moving on. Based on what I know because of the time I spent with the kidnapper and victims in my dreams, I'd say this man has been here no more than thirteen days. When the kidnapper came to the man last night, he brought food. He also made a comment about his time being near, but it didn't sound like his time was up yet. Besides, why bring the guy food if you're just going to kill him later that same night?"

"Based on what you said, it does seem that the timeline was disrupted." I followed Houston's gaze as he looked around the room. There was no furniture other than a table. I remembered that the kidnapper had left the tray of food on the table, but the tray and the food were gone now.

"I guess we should take him back with us."

Houston walked over to the door and looked outside. "Perhaps, but this isn't my jurisdiction, so maybe I should make a call."

"No," I said with as much force as I could muster. "The monster who killed this man and probably killed the woman and the other man I dreamt of sent me here. I feel like I'm part of whatever is going on. If we turn the body over to someone else, we might get cut out, and I need to know exactly what this all means."

Houston didn't answer right away, but eventually, he called Jake and asked him to bring the rescue board Dani kept in the chopper for search and rescue missions in hard to get to places. Once Jake arrived, the men strapped the body onto the board and carried it back to the chopper. Once the body was secured, we climbed into the bird, and Dani headed back to Rescue. Houston called ahead and alerted the coroner that we were bringing in a murder victim. It appeared that he'd been strangled, and based on our calculations, the man had been dead between fifteen and eighteen hours. I had to admit that I felt bad that things had ended the way they had for this man. I'd been dreaming about him for almost two weeks. Surely I could have done something during that time that might have led to him being rescued before he was killed.

Chapter 4

By the time I returned from walking the dogs the following morning, I had a message from Houston letting me know that while the prints he ran in an effort to identify our murder victim didn't turn up any results, the search had prompted a visit from a team from the CIA, who promptly gathered up the remains and took them away.

"So these men from the CIA, did they mention who the victim was or why they were interested in him?" I asked after I'd returned Houston's call.

"No, they simply showed up at my office, showed me their IDs, and then asked where the remains of the murder victim I'd found the previous evening were currently located. I told them the murder victim could be found at the coroner's office, at which point they told me that they were taking custody of the remains and would take over the investigation. They suggested I simply close the case on my end and let them handle things from this point forward."

"Weird."

"It was weird. At first, I wasn't sure the men were who they said they were, but I checked with an FBI buddy of mine, who did some research and confirmed that the men were CIA."

"So is that it?" I asked. "Are you going to close the case as instructed?"

"I guess I am. I no longer have the body, and we didn't find anything at the scene that would help with an investigation, so I don't have much to go on anyway. I suspect that the victim may either be a member of the CIA or perhaps someone of interest to the CIA. Either way, I doubt it's in my best interest to get in the way."

"Yeah." I blew out a breath. "I can see that."

"Did you dream about the man we decided must be the killer last night?" Houston wondered.

"No. I usually don't dream about the man once a victim is dead until, of course, he takes a new victim, at which point the dreams resume in a new location."

"And how long would you say is typical between victims?" Houston asked.

"A couple weeks at least."

"And do you know for certain that the first two victims you witnessed as captives are dead?"

I paused to consider this. "No, not really. I didn't witness the murders, nor did I connect with the kidnapper after I stopped dreaming about the victims while they were still alive. The man we found last night is the first kidnap victim I know who, for a fact, is dead. I assume the others are as well. Somehow I don't see the kidnapper simply allowing these people to continue living after holding them for two to three weeks."

"Yeah," Houston agreed. "I suspect that you're right. I do find it odd, however, that we never found a match for any of the victims in the missing persons files or the unsolved murder files."

"Maybe all the victims are CIA or somehow related to the CIA. Maybe they're keeping things quiet for some reason."

"Perhaps. If that's the case, I doubt we'll ever know for certain."

As frustrating as that was, I supposed it was true. I'd spent time with these individuals in my dreams, and even though my connection was with the kidnapper and not the victims, I still felt invested in the outcome of whatever occurred after these individuals stopped showing up in my dreams. I didn't suppose I could do anything about the fact that these individuals would likely never be known to me, but I found the whole thing increasingly frustrating the more I thought about things.

"I should get going," I said after we'd pretty much wrapped up our conversation. "I was supposed to cover the early shift at the shelter, but I was so late getting home last night that I asked Serena to cover for me. In exchange, I agreed to go in this afternoon for a couple hours so she could leave early."

"Do you think that's a good idea?" Houston asked. "I mean, it does seem at least possible that the person who left the message for you was at the shelter yesterday."

I furrowed my brow. "I guess it's possible that whoever gave Rose the message to give to me was at the shelter yesterday, but I doubt it. And I really doubt that even if that individual had been present at the shelter yesterday, he's still there today. Now that the CIA has come into town and taken the body of his most recent victim, I suspect the kidnapper has moved on."

"Perhaps, but watch your back. We simply don't know at this point whether your connection with the suspected killer puts you in any real danger or not."

I agreed to keep my eyes open and then hung up. I really doubted that the man I'd been channeling would give me directions to his latest victim and then stick around to see whether we'd figure out who he was and arrest him. If the man had any sense at all, he was long gone by this point. Still, I did find it odd that he'd engaged with me to the point of directing me to his latest victim. That part didn't make a lick of sense. It would have provided him more time to make his escape had he not provided the clue he had. And what about the first two victims? What had happened to them? And were there only two? I'd only dreamt about two victims prior to the man whose body we'd found in the cabin, but that didn't mean that the man who'd been responsible for his death hadn't killed others before I began to connect with him.

I had to admit that just considering all the possible variables was giving me a headache. I needed to grab a shower before heading into town, so I gathered some clean clothes and headed into the bathroom. I felt odd wearing another bright colored sweater after the killer had commented on my yellow sweater the previous day, so after I'd showered and dried my hair, I replaced the bright blue sweater I'd initially picked out with a black t-shirt to go with my black jeans, then I slipped my feet into a newer pair of Nikes and grabbed my jacket. I assured the animals I wouldn't be late as I headed out the door.

"Thanks for coming in," Serena said when I arrived. "I know you must be exhausted after your ordeal yesterday, but I promised my sister I'd do a video conference with the whole family."

"Your sister in Ohio?"

"No, the sister who lives in West Virginia. She's the oldest sister and third oldest child. After my dad died, she decided that our family was too spread out and that we'd come to regret not being more active in each other's lives if we didn't make more of a point to stay in touch, and she suggested these video conferences. I wasn't a huge fan of the idea at first, but everyone else got on board, so I figured I should as well."

"And why weren't you a fan of the idea?" I asked.

She shrugged. "I don't know. The whole thing is sort of awkward. I love my siblings, but not only am I the youngest, but I'm only a half-sibling. I know my siblings care about me and want me to be part of the family, but there are times when I feel like an outcast. Both my brothers and all three of my sisters are married with children. They not only seem to have a lot in common with each other, but they're all really settled, if you know what I mean."

"I do. The fact that your siblings have careers and families while you're still struggling to figure out your place in the world probably makes it feel like they're the parents and you're the child."

"That's totally true at times. My dad had a full life before he met my mom. He had five children, a successful career, and a wife he loved. She passed away, he then met and married my mother, and the two of them decided to come north to Alaska. I barely even know my siblings. My parents made sure we visited everyone at least once a year when I was growing up, but visiting older siblings isn't the same as growing up in the same house as them."

"I totally get it," I said.

"And then there's the age difference. I have nieces and nephews who are older than I am. It's a huge joke that Aunt Serena is only in her twenties, and my oldest niece is thirty-two."

"So, do you have grandnieces and nephews?" I wondered.

"No, not yet. Most of my nieces and nephews have big lives and big careers. My oldest brother has two daughters, Gwen and Prescott. Gwen is a doctor, and Prescott is a stockbroker. Neither are married."

"And do your other nieces and nephews live similar lives?"

She nodded. "There's an artist, a small business owner, a political aide, and a law student in the mix. There are also a handful of nieces and nephews who are younger than I am, so that's something. My youngest niece is just five." Serena smiled. "She's actually the family member I enjoy the most."

I gave Serena a hug. "Just keep in mind that you are pretty awesome yourself. You not only run an animal shelter, but you plan to specialize in wild animal rehabilitation. And you live in Alaska. That's pretty badass."

She grinned. "I guess it is. Thanks, Harm. I know my life isn't a competition with my siblings, but I will admit that sometimes when they all get to talking about the important and demanding lives they lead, I feel like a toddler just trying to keep up."

"Just be you because you, my friend, are pretty darn awesome."

Serena grabbed her bag and headed out the door. I hoped she had a pleasant conversation with her family. It would be odd to not only be so much younger than your siblings but so disconnected as well.

After Serena left, I headed over to chat with the men working on the wild animal addition. The last time I'd been in, there had been a new man with the crew who I hadn't met before, which wasn't all that odd since the contractor we'd hired seemed to send whichever temps he had available on any given day.

"Afternoon, guys," I said to the three men Mickey had sent over today. I noticed that two of the men were the same men who'd been here yesterday, but the third man was new. "My name is Harmony," I greeted the man. "I don't think we've met before."

"Stu." The man held out a hand. "I'm new. Today is my first day."

"Welcome. I'm glad to have you onboard." I then looked toward Steve, who seemed to be the only laborer who showed up with any sort of regularity. "What happened to Victor?"

Steve answered. "Victor didn't work out. He was here one day and then didn't show up this morning. It happens, especially when Mickey has to use temps for a job."

"I see. I guess I understand that." I glanced at Doug. He was fairly new, but it seemed as if he'd been around for a couple weeks, so maybe he'd work out.

"I don't want you to worry about the fluid workforce," Steve said. "I've been here since the first day, and I'll be here until the end. I think this project is important for the town. The whole area, really. Your idea is ambitious, but if you can pull it off, I think you'll really make a difference."

"That's what I'm hoping. We do what we can for the wild animals who are brought in, but our resources are limited. Wild animal cages are going to allow us to house the bears, wolves, and caribou who are brought in for the long term if necessary."

"Don't forget about the moose population," Steve said. "I housed one in my barn the winter before last."

I smiled. "I won't forget the moose population. I've housed a few in my barn as well."

I chatted with Steve for a few more minutes and then retired to the office. I tried to remember what I could about the man who'd only been a temp with Summit Contracting for one day. The day I'd worn the yellow sweater. He hadn't spoken, so I had no idea if his voice was deep and raspy, as the voice of the man in my dreams and the man who'd kidnapped Rose had been. But he had been tallish. I couldn't say exactly how tall, but I guessed around six feet. I thought I remembered dark hair. Rose hadn't seen the color of the hair of the man who'd kidnapped her, and I hadn't seen the hair of the man I'd been channeling in my dreams, so I wasn't sure if dark hair was a match or not, but given the entire situation, I felt the man was a candidate.

I wasn't sure if it worked for Victor to have been the one to have kidnapped Rose in terms of a timeline, but I did think it was worth taking a closer look. My first step was to call Mickey to see what I could find out about the guy.

"Victor was a temp," Mickey said once I had him on the line. "As you know, I've been trying to juggle several large projects, so I've had to do some mixing and matching with the shelter project. It hasn't been easy to get the help I need, so I've taken to sending different men with Steve each day. Victor was a real disappointment. He came in looking for work, and he seemed to have a background in construction. Victor was the quiet sort who seemed like he might keep his head down and do his shift without any problems, so I hired him. Steve said he did a good job yesterday. I really hoped the guy would stick, but he didn't show up today."

"Did he leave a forwarding address?"

"Nope. He hasn't come by to pick up his wages for the work he did yesterday. It's always been hard to get and keep qualified laborers, but I've never had one who simply disappeared after one day."

"How about his hire paperwork? Did he give you contact information when he was hired?"

"No. Like I said, he was a temp. You'll need to check with them."

Which is exactly what I did, but when I called the temp agency and spoke to the woman in charge, she told me that she'd never hired a contractor named Victor Bell. She also said that she hadn't sent anyone to Summit on the day in question and had no idea who the man might have been, but he wasn't one of hers. I called Mickey back, who simply told me that the man showed up yesterday saying he was from the temp agency. Mickey said he needed a body and had no reason to doubt Victor, so he sent him with Steve and Doug for the day. If the guy hadn't been sent by the temp agency, he had no idea where he'd come from.

It was at this point that I decided to call Houston.

Chapter 5

Houston suggested that I come by his office to discuss the possibility that Victor could be the kidnapper, which I agreed to do once I closed the shelter for the day. The shelter was open until five o'clock, and it was already after four by this point, so I went to work feeding the animals. We'd had two volunteers come by earlier in the day to clean cages, so that job wouldn't need to be done again until the following day.

"Guess the guys and I will wrap up for the day," Steve said to me as his crew headed out the front door to the parking lot.

"I'll lock up behind you. It's about quitting time anyway," I said.

Steve tilted his hat and assured me he'd be back bright and early in the morning. He really was a hard worker, and we were lucky that he'd been assigned to our project.

Looking at the feeding chart, I confirmed that nothing had changed, so I began filling dishes.

"Hey, Gunther," I said to an old lab who'd come to us after his owner had passed. "I hoped you'd have found a new family by now, but it looks like we're going to need to up our effort to find just the right human for you."

Gunther put his head in my lap as I squatted down to greet him. I'd take him home myself, but I already had more animals than could reasonably fit in my small cabin as it was. What Gunther needed was an older owner, someone who was looking for companionship but wouldn't care that the old dog no longer liked to run and play as he once had. I thought about my friends as I paused to spend a few minutes with the dog. None seemed quite right. Sarge didn't currently have a dog, but he spent most of his time at Neverland, and there were always dogs hanging out there. Still, Sarge did go home at night, and once he left the place where he spent the majority of his time, he was alone. Making a decision, I called him.

"Hey, Sarge, it's Harmony. Listen, I need a favor."

"Anything for you, doll."

"I have a dog. An older lab. I need someone to foster him until I can find a permanent placement."

"Should have known the favor would involve one of your strays."

"I know it's a big ask, but the poor guy is just so sweet. And so old. I really hate to leave him here at the shelter. He needs a human to look out for him until I can get him placed. A nurturing human who will understand how to care for an older animal."

Sarge let out a long breath. "Okay. I'm at Neverland. Bring him by. He can stay with me, but only until you find a permanent placement."

"Only until. I really am working on that. It will probably only be a few days."

I felt a little bad about lying to Sarge since it would likely take more than a few days to find a placement for Gunther, but I also really did believe that once Gunther settled in with Sarge, there wouldn't be a need to look further for a home for the old guy. Sarge liked to portray a grizzly front to the world, but once you got to know the man, anyone with a heart could see that he was about as sweet and cuddly as they came.

Grabbing a leash, I called Houston and told him that I needed to drop Gunther off with Sarge before stopping by. He admitted he was hungry and wouldn't mind grabbing a bite to eat, so we agreed to meet at Neverland to discuss Victor Bell and the possibility that he might be the kidnapper over dinner. I wasn't sure that the timeline would even allow for such a thing, but given the fact that he was at the shelter yesterday when I'd been there wearing my yellow sweater and hadn't returned today, I thought it was at least a possibility.

As I'd hoped, Sarge and Gunther loved each other at first sight. I really thought the two would be good for each other. Sarge was an older man who liked to hang out at Neverland but rarely went anywhere other than home, and Gunther was an old but friendly dog who enjoyed occasional cuddles and lots of naps.

"So, what do you think?" I asked Houston after he'd joined me for dinner, and I'd filled him in on my idea that perhaps the man who'd been introduced as Victor Bell might actually have been the same man I'd been sharing thoughts with during my dreams for months now.

"I guess if this man is aware that you're in his head and he's aware of who you are, he might have decided to get a closer look. Theoretically, he might have scoped out the situation and then made the decision to try to get a closer look by signing on with the construction crew. It makes sense that if this had been the case, he would have only shown up that one day. Have you spoken to the man who owns the company you've contracted with?"

"I have. Mickey said that Victor showed up yesterday asking for work. He told Mickey that the temp agency had sent him. Mickey needed laborers, so he sent him to the shelter with Steve and his crew. I was introduced to the man, but I never spoke to him. I was only at the shelter for a couple of hours and didn't pay attention to what the guy was doing.

Mickey said that the guy didn't show up this morning, and when I called the temp agency to ask about it, the woman who runs the place had no idea what I was talking about."

"It does sound as if the man who showed up yesterday might be the one who kidnapped Rose later in the day," Houston said, taking a sip of his beer. "I doubt that Victor Bell is the guy's real name, but I'll run it. I don't suppose you have a photo."

"No. Sorry. There was no reason to take one. I can describe the guy. Sort of. I mean, I wasn't really paying all that much attention, but I remember that the guy was around six feet tall and had dark hair. Beyond that, I don't remember much. I seem to remember that all three men were wearing denim pants. I suppose we can talk to Steve and Doug to see if they remember more about the guy since they spent the day with him."

Houston got his cell phone out and made a note. "I'll call both men when we're done here." Houston nodded toward the bar area where Gunther was curled up next to Sitka. "It looks like Sitka has a new buddy."

"Gunther is a dog from the shelter I asked Sarge to foster."

"By 'foster,' I assume you mean 'adopt,' and by 'asked,' I assume you mean 'tricked.'"

"Basically."

"I get it, and I agree that the pair seem suited. I absolutely adore Kojak, and I'm sure I wouldn't have him if you hadn't persuaded me to take a chance and give him a home. I just hope Sarge and Gunther are as happy as Kojak and I are."

Once we finished our meal, Houston called and spoke to both Steve and Doug. Both had small items to add about how the man looked or what he said, but neither had heard or observed anything that would help us to track the guy down. I supposed if we knew that Victor was actually the person who'd kidnapped Rose, that would fill in a few of the blanks, but it wouldn't help us find him. And maybe finding him wasn't our job. The CIA seemed to think Houston should just let it go. Maybe he should. It's not like we had a lead to follow anyway.

Chapter 6

By the following day, I'd somehow convinced myself to take my own advice and let the whole thing go. I hadn't dreamt about the kidnapper last evening, and while the previous pattern was to skip dreams on nights the man didn't seem to have a captive, I still allowed myself to believe that this particular nightmare was really over.

I had an off day today, which made things even better. I didn't have a shift at either the animal shelter or Neverland, so as long as I wasn't called in for a rescue, I should be able to take the dogs for an extra-long walk and then see to some chores I'd been meaning to take care of around the property. The snow had completely melted now that the days had grown long, and the temperatures had increased a bit. I allowed most of my property to grow naturally, but I did have a small patch of dirt where I'd attempted to grow a vegetable garden last year. Of course, with the growing season being so short, the whole thing had been a bust, but I considered doing some research and then trying again this year. If not vegetables, then perhaps a few hearty annuals to add some color. Of course, even if I could get the dang things planted, I'd probably kill them within a week. I had a tendency to forget about the garden when I got overly busy. I never forgot about my animals and always tended to their needs or made arrangements for someone else to do it in my stead, but flowers planted in the yard had never experienced much of a life expectancy.

When the dogs and I arrived at the lake, rather than turning them around as I'd done all week, I gave them the command to run and play. Most of the dogs took me up on my offer, although Lucky decided that a nap in the shade was more his cup of tea. Once the dogs had swam to their heart's content and had wandered over to where Lucky and I waited, I got up from my seat on a log I'd found and headed back to the cabin. When Denali let out a happy yip and then took off running, I knew who I'd find waiting for me on my doorstep.

"Shredder!" I enthusiastically greeted the mysterious friend who seemed to drift in and out of my life. "After the CIA showed up yesterday, I should have assumed you'd show up today."

"Given my line of work, it's unfortunate that I'm so predictable," Shredder said as he greeted each of my dogs, all of whom were thrilled to see him. I wasn't really sure why the dogs adored my mysterious friend to the degree that they seemed to. Denali was uber protective and had never warmed up to anyone other than Shredder and me. Denali tolerated both Jake and Houston, and he seemed okay with Justine from the veterinary clinic and Serena from the shelter, but when it came to absolute adoration, he seemed to save that for the bleached blond stranger who looked like he'd just stepped off a surfboard but as far as I could tell seemed to work for some sort of black ops organization.

"Come in," I invited him. "Where's Riptide?" I asked about his dog.

"I left him with a friend since my trip was a last-minute sort of thing, and I wasn't sure where all it would take me."

"I'm sorry he isn't with you, but I completely understand. I need to get the dogs some water, and then you can tell me why you're here."

Shredder followed me into the cabin, much to Denali's delight. I filled all the dog bowls with water, began brewing a pot of coffee, and then I offered Shredder breakfast since I hadn't eaten yet. He accepted my offer, settling onto a bar stool as I began cracking eggs. I expected him to jump right in with questions about the man in the cabin, but instead, he asked about Jake and the gang. I answered that they were all fine. I shared a few little tidbits about each search and rescue team member, and then he asked about Houston.

"He's fine as well. Frustrated that the CIA took over his murder investigation, but otherwise, he's fine."

"Did the two of you ever hook up?"

I paused, half-cracked egg in midair, before answering. "No. Not really. Well, almost."

He quirked a brow.

"It's complicated."

He laughed. "Care to expand?"

Not really, but I supposed I would. "Houston and I had a moment a while back. He asked me if I dated since he'd never seen me date anyone, and I answered that it wasn't that I had anything against dating but that I just hadn't had the opportunity as of late. Then he informed me that he hadn't dated since his divorce, but he was thinking about maybe getting back in the game. He asked if dating was something I'd be interested in when he was ready, and I indicated that it would be. I thought that he'd ask me out at some point after that, but it's been months and months, and so far, nothing. To be fair, he didn't say he was ready, only that he was wondering what I thought about the whole thing once he was."

"So maybe you should ask him out," Shredder suggested as I poured the eggs in a pan.

"I don't think I'm willing to do that. The whole thing feels sort of awkward, and I guess I'm concerned about what would happen if we did date and it didn't work out. We're such great friends, and we work together fairly often. I'd hate for anything to interfere with that." I picked up a loaf of bread and began settling slices in the toaster. "There's juice in the refrigerator if you want some."

Shredder got up and poured us each a glass of juice. He set the glasses on the table and then walked over to the stove where I was scrambling the eggs. He put an arm around my shoulders. "You know I love you, and you know I would never intentionally say anything to hurt you, but in this case, I really believe you're overthinking things."

"Overthinking things? This isn't a game. It's important."

He pulled me close to his side and kissed me on the forehead. "I know it's not a game, but sometimes you just have to know what you want and go for it. It's not easy to allow yourself to fall in love, and at times doing so leads to heartbreak, but love tried and lost really is better than spending the rest of your life wondering what might have been."

I began scraping eggs onto plates. "It sounds as if you've been in love at some point in your past."

"I have."

"And since in all the time I've known you, you've never mentioned having a girl, I assume you lost this woman at some point along the way."

"I did."

I set the plates on the table and then grabbed the butter for the toast.

"And in your opinion, loving and losing is better than having never loved at all."

He sat down at the table. "I think it might be. There was a woman I loved a while back who, given my job, I kept at a distance. We were friends, but as time passed, I found that I wanted something more. The problem was that by the time I finally came to terms with my own feelings, she'd found another guy. They are happily married with children now. Looking back, if I had it to do over again, I'd have done things differently."

I had to admit that this conversation surprised me. Shredder was this mysterious guy whose real name I didn't even know, but despite the intensity of his job, he seemed sort of relaxed and easy-going. If he'd told me that he'd never been in love, I wouldn't have been surprised. To find that he had been, only to lose the woman by not acting on his feelings, served to cement in my mind the fact that I really didn't know the man at all.

"So let's discuss Alfred Summerton," Shredder said, changing the subject.

"Alfred Summerton?" I asked.

"The man whose body was in your morgue before my buddies from the CIA confiscated it."

"So you know what's going on," I said.

He nodded. "I do, but before I share what I know with you, I need you to tell me how Houston ended up with him in the first place."

I decided to start at the beginning. I described how I'd first dreamt of a woman being held in a warehouse several months ago. At the time, I thought the dream was just a dream, but as time went by, I began to suspect that my late-night visits to this warehouse might be something more. I informed Shredder that I'd shared my dreams with Houston, who agreed to search for a missing person matching the description of the woman from my dreams, but that his search had come up empty. Shredder asked about the location of the warehouse, and I answered that I didn't know. "It was just a warehouse in an area filled with warehouses. Nothing really stood out as being unique."

"A few weeks after my dreams featuring the woman began, they just stopped. I went through a period of about three weeks with no dreams, but then they started up again. This time, the victim was a man being held in a shed near a lake. I saw enough to know that the landscape didn't look like Alaska, but I had no idea where either the lake or the shed were located. As with my dreams about the woman, my dreams about this man continued for a few weeks before stopping. As before, there was a break in my dreams, and when they started up again, the kidnapped person was a different man. This time, the man was locked in a cabin near a river. This landscape looked like Alaska, but I wasn't sure where the cabin was located.

I shared with Shredder that I was still trying to figure all this out when a woman was taken from the local market. The search and rescue team had been activated, and we'd found her before any real damage was done. The kidnapper seemed to have taken her in order to deliver a message to me. I shared the content of the message and the fact that the killer commented about the yellow sweater I'd been wearing earlier in the day. This had Shredder frowning.

I took Shredder through the retrieval of the body up to the point where the CIA had shown up and confiscated it.

"So that's what I know," I said. "Now it's your turn. What in the heck is going on, and how is it that I'm involved in this whole thing?"

Shredder got up and refilled his coffee cup before he answered. "Four months ago, an agent for MI6 went missing. I have reason to believe the woman who went missing is the same woman you saw being held in the warehouse during your first set of dreams. I'll pull up a photo in a minute so we can confirm this. I think that what is important to this discussion is that the woman simply disappeared, and no one we've talked to, other than you, has claimed to have seen her since."

"I didn't really see her," I pointed out. "Not in person. And even if it is the same person, it's been weeks since it appears the killer moved on."

"Yes." Shredder frowned. "It does sound that way. I hoped you knew what happened to her after the warehouse, but it sounds like the dreams featuring this woman just ended, and when they started back up, there was a different hostage."

"That's it exactly," I said. "I really don't know if these people are dead or alive at this point. I suspect they're dead, but I really don't know that."

"Do you think you can intentionally connect with them?" Shredder asked. "Assuming they're still alive, of course."

I paused. "I'm not sure. I haven't actually tried that."

"Would you be willing to?"

I nodded. "I can try. Having a photo will help. So what can you tell me about the other two hostages? The man I saw in the shed and the one whose body we found in the cabin?"

"I believe the man you saw in the shed is a missing agent from Interpol. I will confirm this in a minute, but this man has been missing for a couple months, so he fits the timeline. The man you found in the cabin is a CIA agent who's been missing for a little over two weeks. The CIA has been looking for him, but admittedly not in Alaska. They likely would never have found him if Houston hadn't run the prints looking for a match."

"So this man who I seem to have had the misfortune of psychically connecting with has kidnapped and probably killed agents for MI6, Interpol, and the CIA. Why?"

"That is the question the organization I work with is trying to answer. We believe the victims were targeted and not random, however. It has even been suggested that the man behind these disappearances has a list he's working from. So far, we haven't been able to verify this, and we have no idea why these specific individuals have been targeted. Honestly, the man you found in the cabin and your connection with the others is the only lead we have."

Great. I suddenly had a feeling my whole day off wasn't going to be much of a day off at all. "You know I'll help if I can. What do you need me to do?"

"First, I'm going to do the dishes while you take care of the animals in the barn. That is what you planned to do next if I hadn't shown up, isn't it?"

I nodded. "You know me well. That is exactly what I planned to do next, and Homer will be wanting his breakfast. And when I'm done with that?"

"I'm going to show you photos of the MI6 agent, as well as the agent from Interpol. If you're able to confirm that these are indeed the individuals who showed up in your dreams, then we'll see if you can connect with them. I realize that it's a long shot, but at this point, it's the only shot we have."

"Okay," I said as I stood up. "I'll head out to the barn and take care of Homer and the rabbits. If you're planning on staying, you can take your stuff into the guest room. The bedding is clean, and the door has been closed, so the animal hair should be minimal."

"Let's see how things go this afternoon, and then I'll decide whether I'll be staying."

I shrugged. "Suit yourself, but if you take off too soon, you're going to break Denali's heart."

He bent down and ruffed the wolf hybrid behind the ears. "I'll keep that in mind. I really have missed the big guy."

I wasn't sure exactly how Denali and Shredder were connected, but they were. The dog, who didn't really like anyone other than me, had adored him on sight, and he always seemed to know when Shredder was around, even if he'd yet to announce himself. I supposed Denali's total acceptance of Shredder was the reason I'd decided to trust him the first time we met. Denali had discriminating taste, so if he trusted the man, then who was I not to? Since I'd first met Shredder, I'd learned to accept the fact that while he would always be one of the most important people in my life, he would also be the sort to pop in and out without any notice or explanation. I wondered about the woman he'd been in love with. Had she been an agent living the same lifestyle as he, or had she been someone he'd met in passing and had formed an attachment to? I supposed I'd never know, and maybe it really didn't matter.

Chapter 7

Once the animals had been taken care of, I sat down on the sofa and got as comfortable as I could. Shredder provided me a photo of the surprisingly young and pretty MI6 agent. I spent a few minutes committing her face to memory before closing my eyes, picturing her image, and focusing on her name.

Charlotte Brentwood.

I tried to relax and be receptive to any feedback I might receive. In the early years, when I was still trying to figure out how to use my gift, I was only able to "see" those individuals I was meant to help during a rescue. The connection was a one-way sort of thing where I could see them, but they couldn't see or feel me. This gift was useful in determining where a lost hiker or skier might be, but the use of the gift was limited to certain situations. As time went by, I not only began to see the victim I was destined to save but to feel their emotions as well. This gave the S&R team additional information, which aided in the rescue, but was also harder on me, causing me to lose a bit of myself with each rescue.

My ability to connect has continued to evolve as time has gone by. At some point, I realized that not only was I able to see and feel the person I was connected with, but they could hear and feel me as well. I began to connect with individuals in other ways as well. The more practice I had psychically connecting with others, the better I became and the more control I seemed to have over who I connected with. Once I was able to psychically communicate with those I connected with at will, things got a lot easier. It helped when those the team had set out to find were able to actually tell us where they were and what condition they were in physically.

I think I would have been happy if my gift had stopped evolving at this point. These connections took a lot out of me, but I felt good that my ability was helping to save lives. But then I began to connect, not only with the victims the team had set out to save but with the killers who telegraphed so much pain into the airways as they worked toward their ultimate revenge that I couldn't help but get tangled up with this raw and unfocused energy.

I supposed my new ability to connect with individuals during my sleeping hours would, at some point, be the end of me. There were times when my mind was at peace and letting REM sleep occur, but more and more often, it seemed that I woke up from my dream-filled slumber even more exhausted than when I'd gone to bed.

Intentionally trying to connect with individuals after a long night of vivid dreams was exhausting. There were times when I wasn't sure I'd survive the experience, but I knew how important it was and hated to let down those individuals in my life who asked me to try.

"I'm not getting anything," I said after several minutes. "Keep in mind that I can only connect if the person is alive and conscious." I opened my eyes and looked at Shredder. "I'm afraid that there's a good chance this woman is dead."

He blew out a breath. "Yeah, I know. I just felt it was important to try. What about Dillinger Craig?"

I looked at his image and committed it to memory before closing my eyes and focusing on his image and name. I was fairly sure that he was dead as well since I hadn't dreamt of him in weeks, but I supposed it would give both Shredder and me peace of mind to at least try to connect in the event he hadn't yet been killed.

When I was unable to get even a blip after more than twenty minutes, Shredder agreed that it was probably best that I save my energy. I felt so bad for Shredder, who seemed to have known these individuals in some capacity. He told me he needed to make a call, and I suggested that he head outdoors since the signal was sketchy inside the cabin but not all that bad standing out in the drive.

When Shredder came back in, I decided to talk to him about allowing Houston and Jake in on the whole thing. I supposed it was likely that this particular serial killer had moved on from Alaska, and tracking him down would fall to Shredder and the group he worked for rather than local law enforcement, but since I was involved, I knew that Houston would want to be involved, and keeping both Houston and Jake in the loop would certainly make my life a lot easier.

"So what do these individuals have in common?" I asked Shredder while we waited for Houston to arrive at my cabin after Shredder agreed that I could call and invite him over. "You mentioned a list. Why would these three individuals be on the list? I get that they all work for intelligence agencies and that links them, but there are a lot of people who work for intelligence agencies around the world, so why these three?"

"I'm not sure," Shredder admitted. "When Charlotte Brentwood went missing, we all just assumed that whoever had taken her had a beef with her specifically. My agency wasn't involved at this point since MI6 was taking care of the search for Charlotte in-house, but I'd met Charlotte in the past, so when I heard what had happened, I decided to follow the investigation. As I've indicated, she never has shown up, so I suppose we can't know with a hundred percent certainty that Charlotte is dead or even that she was taken by the same person who took the others, but given what I know at this point, it seems likely."

"Was she taken from her home?" I asked

Shredder shook his head. "The last time anyone saw her, she was in Ukraine. I don't know specifically where in Ukraine since MI6 is keeping the details of her mission to themselves, but I suspect she was there to gather intel on recent movement within the Russian government to expand their territory."

"And Dillinger Craig?" I asked. "Where was he when he was last seen?"

"I'm not sure. Interpol is keeping what they know close to the vest. All I know is that Dillinger, like Charlotte, seems to be missing. He hasn't been answering communications and has failed to check in with his superiors for almost two months. No one knows what happened to him."

"And Alfred Summerton?" I asked.

"I know he worked for the CIA, and before showing up here in Alaska, he was last seen in Prague. No one knows how he ended up in Alaska, and as far as anyone I've spoken to knows, he shouldn't have been anywhere near the location where his body was found."

"So he may have been taken from somewhere other than Alaska and brought here."

"That's the most popular opinion at this point."

"Again, I have to ask why."

Shredder just shrugged.

Houston showed up with his dog, Kojak, at this point, so I took a few minutes to greet him and catch him up on our conversation.

"So you only became involved in this after I did the fingerprint search?" he asked Shredder.

"That is correct," Shredder answered. "As I mentioned to Harmony, I know Charlotte, so I had been following the investigation into her disappearance since the beginning in an unofficial capacity. The organization I work for wasn't officially brought into the loop, however, until you did the fingerprint search, and we realized that you had a missing CIA agent in your morgue."

"And who exactly do you work for?" Houston asked.

"I really can't say, but I can assure you that we are the good guys."

Houston's lips tightened. I think it bothered him that Shredder was so mysterious, but the mysterious man had helped us out in the past, so I doubted he'd fuss too much.

"I tried to connect with the missing MI6 agent, as well as the missing Interpol agent, but didn't pick anything up," I informed Houston. "Given the fact that I had been able to see them in my dreams at one point, I'm going to assume that they're dead."

"But their bodies still haven't shown up," Houston confirmed.

Shredder indicated that Houston was correct in his assertion.

"So, where does this leave us now?" Houston asked. "I have an open murder case that I'd very much like to close despite the fact that the men from the CIA who took Alfred Summerton's body instructed me to leave the whole thing alone."

Shredder gave Houston a look of sympathy. "I get the fact that it's hard to let someone else take over a murder case that you've been involved in, but in the opinion of those I work with, the man who killed Alfred has likely moved on, and it's unlikely he will return to Alaska."

"You said it was the opinion of those you work with that this man has moved on," Houston pointed out. "What is your opinion on the matter?"

Shredder hesitated before he answered. "Honestly, I'm less certain that this killer has moved on. He seemed to have kidnapped, and most likely killed, the first two victims without involving anyone else. In my opinion, any man who has the skill set to get the upper hand on both Charlotte and Dillinger has to be specially trained. Maybe special forces. Perhaps a black ops agency. Or possibly even ex-intelligence. The man I'm imagining would work alone. He'd get in and out and do what needed to be done without leaving one bit of evidence behind. But the series of events that took place yesterday seems to break that mold. This man intentionally sought out Harmony. He pulled her into his story. In my opinion, the man isn't done with her."

"So, do you think he's still here in Alaska?" Houston asked.

"I think that is a distinct possibility. My orders are to head out tonight, but I don't feel right leaving with things so unresolved."

"I have to admit that given the fact that this killer seems to have fixated on Harmony, I'd prefer you stay." Houston looked at me. "You did fill him in on the man at the shelter, didn't you?"

"Man at the shelter?" Shredder asked.

I went on to explain that it was possible that the man I'd been dreaming about had shown up in person at the shelter. This caused Shredder's brow to furrow deeply.

Houston's cell phone rang just as I was about to suggest we sit down and come up with a strategy. He headed outside, spoke to someone for less than a minute, and then returned. "We have another kidnapping. This time, the victim is a seven-year-old named Henry Wallace. He was taken by a man in a blue shirt, who showed up at the park where he was playing."

"Was he there with an adult?" I asked.

Houston nodded. "His mother was sitting on a bench not all that far away from where he was playing. She witnessed the whole thing, but it happened so fast that she barely remembers any details. I need to go." He called Kojak.

"I'll come with you," I said. "Just in case. If I can make a connection, maybe we can figure out where to search."

"Okay. We'll take my truck. You can call Jake while we make the trip to the park. It might be a good idea to put the S&R team on standby."

I glanced at Shredder. "Will you be here when we return?"

"I'm honestly not sure. I'm waiting for a call from my boss. I guess it depends on how that goes. If I'm not here when you return, that will most likely mean that my request to stay was denied."

I stepped forward and hugged the man in the event he was ordered to leave and then headed out the door with Houston. "Do you think this is the same man from yesterday?" I asked Houston as we sped toward the park where Jake, as well as Houston's men, were supposed to meet us.

"I don't know. I feel like it must be related, but a witness told the emergency dispatcher that the man who grabbed the child was about five feet six or seven inches tall. The witness also said that the man was driving a white truck with Alaska plates. I suppose our kidnapper may have stolen a vehicle or even rented one, but when I spoke to Rose yesterday, she told me that the man who kidnapped her drove a black four-wheel-drive truck with Minnesota plates."

"Minnesota plates? Why would he have a truck with Minnesota plates?"

Houston shrugged. "I have no idea. We never did find or identify the truck. Rose remembered the state but couldn't remember the license plate number."

There hadn't been a vehicle of any sort at the cabin where we'd found Alfred Summerton's body, which given the fact that the killer was no longer in the area, made perfect sense. Of course, the killer would have had a vehicle when he kidnapped Rose. I'm not sure why I hadn't stopped to wonder about this before. I guess Houston must have thought to ask about a vehicle at some point, but the subject of a vehicle hadn't come up while I was present in the conversation.

By the time we arrived at the park, Houston's two deputies were already there. The witness and the mother were both sequestered off to the side, giving their statements to the deputies. Houston made his way toward the short blond with the blunt cut, who was crying hysterically.

"Are you Henry's mother?" Houston asked.

"I am. You have to find my baby. He's just a little boy. Who would do such a thing?"

"We're going to do everything we can to find him, ma'am. Do you happen to have a photo of him with you?"

She nodded and walked over to a bench where a large leather purse had been left unattended. She pulled a red leather wallet out and opened it. After pulling a small photo out, she handed it to Houston.

"This is pretty recent. I guess it was taken three or four months ago."

"And what did Henry have on today?" Houston asked.

"A blue sweatshirt, red Flash t-shirt, and blue jeans. Do you have any idea where to look for him?"

Houston looked at me. I took the photo he offered and headed toward the truck. I knew my making a connection with the child who must be terrified by this point would be more likely if I had a quiet place to work.

"Okay, Henry," I said to myself once I was settled in the truck with the photo. "Let's see if we can get you home safely."

It took nearly fifteen minutes, but eventually, I was able to get through to the child. I could hear someone talking in the background. The voice was male but high-pitched. It didn't sound at all like the voice I'd been dreaming about for the past several months. The voice was gentle yet impatient. The man kept telling the child to stop crying, but, of course, the child was terrified and screamed even louder. I didn't think Henry was aware of my presence at this point, but I knew if I could get his attention, I might be able to give him instructions that would help us find him.

"Henry, my name is Harmony," I said in my mind, hoping he would begin to sense me. "I'm going to help you, but you need to help me."

The boy continued to scream and cry, and unfortunately, he was looking down, so while I could sense that he was still traveling in the truck, I couldn't see any of the scenery as it passed by.

"Do you believe in superheroes?" I asked in my mind.

The boy stopped crying for just a second and looked around.

"I'm not there in the truck with you. I can communicate telepathically, just like a superhero. If you want to ask me a question, just think about it in your mind. Don't say it out loud, however. We don't want the bad man to know."

"You can see me?" Henry asked.

"I can see what you see. I need you to look up and look out the window."

The boy did as I instructed. "Good. Very good. It looks like you're traveling north along the highway. I know you are scared, but I am going to come for you. I need you to keep looking out the window."

"Okay," the boy said out loud.

"Okay, what?" the driver of the truck asked.

"Shh," I said. "Don't talk out loud to me. Only in your mind."

"Okay," the boy answered with his thoughts.

"I'm going to take a short break while I get my friend, the police chief. We're going to come for you right now. All I need you to do is keep looking out the window so I can see where you are. I may ask you questions, so listen for me in your mind."

"Okay."

"Like I just said, I'm going to need to break the connection for just a couple minutes while I get the police, but I'll be right back."

"Okay."

I hated to break the connection for even a moment, but I knew that the moment I opened my eyes, the connection would be gone. I quickly opened the door and went for Houston. I informed him that I knew where to look. He instructed his men to follow us. When Henry's mother insisted on coming along, Jake offered to bring her along in his truck.

"Is he okay?" Houston asked as we sped along the highway.

"He's scared but unharmed. I need to connect again to let him know I'm still here."

Houston nodded, and I closed my eyes and focused. When I finally reconnected, I could see that the truck the boy was riding in had turned off the highway. I frantically looked around for a landmark. Luckily, there was a familiar mountain in the background.

"I see you turned off the road," I said in my mind.

"Can you still find me?"

"I can. I'm on my way. At this point, I just need you to keep looking out the window."

I could sense that the boy was beginning to panic, so I told him that not only was I on my way, but the police, along with his mother, were coming for him as well. When I mentioned his mother, he seemed to calm down a bit.

"Turn off on the hunting road that leads out to the old homestead at the foot of Perishing Mountain," I said, keeping my eyes closed in an attempt to keep the connection. "The man driving the truck Henry is riding in has stopped. Henry is beginning to cry again. I think the man in the truck is at the homestead."

I tried to calm Henry, but he was hysterical again. The child had his eyes closed and was thrashing around, so I couldn't get a good look at things. I tried to calm him once more, but he cried even louder. I could feel my heart begin to race as the connection was broken.

"I lost him," I said.

"Lost him? Why?" Houston asked.

"I'm not sure. Henry was really upset, and he may have pushed me out. I suppose it's also possible that the man he's with knocked him out in order to quiet him down." I swallowed hard. "Of course, there's also the possibility that..." I left the thought unfinished.

"Don't even go there," Houston said, speeding up a bit more.

When we reached the road where Houston needed to turn, we were both a bundle of nerves. The dirt road was rutted, but we made our way toward the old homestead as quickly as possible. When we finally arrived at the homestead, we found Henry lying on the back seat of a white truck that had been left near an outbuilding. The man who'd been driving the truck was nowhere in sight. I had to assume he'd had another vehicle waiting in which he made his escape.

My heart stopped for an instant when I first saw the child on the back seat of the white truck, but once I had the chance to get a closer look, I could see that he was alive.

"He's breathing but unconscious," I said to Houston. "He has a bump on his head. I suspect the kidnapper knocked him out. We should get him to the hospital."

Henry's mother arrived as Houston was pulling his cell phone out to call Dani. He asked her to bring Jordan and pick up Henry and his mother. By the time Dani and Jordan arrived, Henry was awake and happily wrapped in his mother's arms.

"So, what do you think that was all about?" I asked Houston and Jake once Dani had taken off with Jordan, Henry, and Henry's mother. "Why would this guy kidnap this kid, bring him all the way out here, and then just leave him behind when he made his getaway? The whole thing had to be planned, but I really don't see a motive."

"I have no idea," Houston said. He glanced toward the truck. "Maybe we can get some prints. I'm not sure that identifying our kidnapper will tell us everything we need, but it is a place to start."

Chapter 8

Houston and I spent over an hour at the homestead after Dani left with Henry and his mother. The truck was towed back to the police station, and the area around the truck was thoroughly searched and photographed. By the time we got back to my cabin, it was late. I wondered if Shredder had taken the dogs out for a walk and left his cell phone behind since he hadn't answered when I'd called, nor had he replied to the text I sent as an update. I was surprised to find all the dogs inside the cabin when I arrived. They all dashed to the door in greeting, but Shredder was nowhere in sight. I supposed he might have received his new orders and left before I made it home, but it seemed as if he would have at least left me a message.

"Denali," I called to the dog who'd dashed out the door as soon as I opened it.

I could hear him barking frantically. I supposed that if Shredder left, Denali might be looking for him. I called again, and this time, Denali came back.

"I'm sorry, buddy," I said to the dog. "I know he wasn't here long, but you know that he tends to pop in and out unannounced. Maybe he'll be back after he does whatever it is he must have been assigned to do."

Denali returned to the cabin as I instructed him to, but he wasn't happy about the current state of affairs.

"I need to get back and file my report about the kidnapping," Houston said to me.

"That's fine. I think I'll see to the animals and then head to Neverland. I've been missing more shifts than I've shown up for lately."

"Maybe I'll stop by later for a bite."

I smiled. "I'd like that."

After I'd taken the dogs out for a quick run, fed everyone, and cleaned the barn and cat box, I jumped into the shower. I pulled jeans and a sweater on, stuffed my feet into comfortable shoes, and then headed out the door. As I drove toward Neverland, I thought about Shredder. I knew I shouldn't be worried. The guy did tend to pop in and out, and he'd told me he was waiting for a call about his next move. I was sure he was simply off to the next location in his journey for answers, but it did seem sort of odd that he hadn't at least texted me back. I supposed I'd try texting him again later.

"You made it in," Jake greeted after I walked in through the front door.

"I'm here and ready to work," I said after hugging Sarge, petting Gunther behind the ear, and then following in kind with Sitka. I tossed a nod at Wyatt, who was working the bar this evening. "It looks like we have a good crowd tonight."

"Sarge made his beef ribs. They've been smoking all day, and since everyone who's come in has ordered a full rack, it seems word got out," Jake informed me.

I loved Sarge's beef ribs. His special secret sauce was to die for. I hoped there would be enough left at the end of my shift to take some home with me. "I'm going to call Harley to let him know we have ribs," I said. "He loves those things, and he may not have heard. Did anyone tell Landon?" I asked about another search and rescue team member.

"I called him," Wyatt said. "He should be here in half an hour or so. He's bringing Dani."

Leave it to Sarge's ribs to get the whole gang together.

After I called Harley and told him about the ribs, I got to work waiting on customers. There were those who wondered why I didn't aspire to a career other than waitressing, but the reality was that I loved my job. Not only was it super flexible, making both my volunteer work with the shelter and the search and rescue team possible, but it was a good way to stay in touch with friends and neighbors since most folks make it in at one point or another.

I was chatting with a group from the volunteer fire department when Landon walked in with Dani. They sat at the bar so they could chat with Wyatt, who was working, and Jordan, who was sipping a glass of wine. I'd called Harley, who assured me that he'd be by with Brittany as soon as they could get ready. I wasn't sure if they'd want to join the gang at the bar or prefer a table for two, so I reserved a table, figuring that if they wanted to sit at the bar, I could simply release the table to the next couple who stopped by.

Houston was trying to track down the man who'd kidnapped the child we'd rescued, so he wouldn't be able to stop by, but he did ask if it was possible for me to set some ribs aside that he could pick up and take back to his office to eat. I agreed to set ribs, beans, and slaw aside, and Jake volunteered to deliver them. I was somewhat surprised by this, but I suspected that Jake's real motivation in playing delivery boy was a desire to have a private chat with Houston. It would allow the men in my life to discuss me and the potential danger I might have landed myself in, given the fact that the man I'd been connecting with had gone to so much trouble to get my attention.

I was somewhat irked by the whole thing, but not irked enough to make an issue of it, so when Jake left with the food, I simply reminded him to grab lots of napkins and sent him on his way.

Harley and Brittany showed up shortly after Jake left with Houston's order. It seemed as if Brittany was hoping for the table for two when offered the choice, but Harley voiced his opinion that he'd prefer to eat at the bar with the gang before she had a chance to say anything. I supposed this bode well for Serena. If Harley considered Brittany to be a romantic partner, he would have asked her which she preferred rather than speaking for the both of them without consulting her.

"I forgot how much I missed these ribs," Harley said after I'd slipped onto an open stool next to him during one of my breaks.

"They are the best ribs in the state."

"Actually, they're the best ribs anywhere. At least the best ribs I've tasted," Harley said.

"Ribs are messy, so I generally avoid them," Brittany said as she nibbled on a salad.

"You have no idea what you're missing," Harley said. He tore off a piece of meat, stuck it with a fork, swirled it around in the extra sauce, and offered it to Brittany.

She accepted the bite and then sighed with delight once she realized what the fuss had been all about.

"Maybe I will take a few ribs on the side," she said. "I never thought to eat them with a fork."

I stifled a laugh as I headed into the kitchen to grab the ribs. Sarge was on the phone chatting with someone about a fundraiser, so I waited until he hung up to put in the order.

"Side of ribs," I said once he was off the phone.

"Coming right up."

"Sounds like you're trying to raise funds for new equipment," I said to Sarge as he made up the plate.

He nodded. "Jake and I talked about it earlier. A lot of the equipment used by the search and rescue team is dated and really needs to be replaced. Of course, replacing it takes cash. A lot of it. I suggested a community-based fundraiser such as a bake sale or community picnic, but Jake thought that might be more trouble than it was worth. He felt that hitting up a few of our wealthier residents might be an easier way to go. In the end, we decided that we really did need a lot of money, so we're going to pursue both angles." He handed me the plate. "Seems like you've been successful raising funds for the shelter. Any tips?"

"The main reason I've been so successful with the shelter is due to Harley's involvement. Not only has he personally donated a lot of money, but he's asked his rich friends to help out as well. The search and rescue team in Rescue serves an important role in the community, so I'll talk to Harley and see if he wants to help with the fund-raising effort."

"Thank you, darlin'. I appreciate that."

I brought Brittany's rib order to her and slipped back onto the stool I'd recently vacated to grab the food. "Sarge and Jake are planning a fundraiser of some sort to raise funds for new equipment for the search and rescue team," I said to Harley. "I don't suppose you want to help. You seem to have a lot of contacts, and we need a lot of funds."

Harley swiped a napkin across his face. "I can help. I'm in town for the summer. Do the guys have a plan at this point?"

"No. They just know a lot of money is needed and are discussing options. If you have any ideas, I know the entire search and rescue team will be in your debt."

"I'm in. Maybe we can meet this week and discuss options."

I put an arm around Harley's neck and kissed his cheek. "Thanks. I'll let Sarge know. Check with him before you leave. I'm sure any day this week will work, but it might be best to confirm that with both Jake and Sarge."

A party of six walked in, so I headed across the room to seat them. Harley really was a valued member of our community even though he was away for half of each year. He'd lived in Rescue as a kid, and I knew he had a connection with the place that went far beyond an adventure seeker's need for the rugged outdoors and a bit of excitement.

I always enjoyed rib nights since it gave me a chance to catch up with everyone, but I was exhausted by the time I got home. I let the dogs out for a quick bathroom break, and then I went directly to bed. I was asleep before my head even hit the pillow. I was pretty sure the man I'd been channeling was between kidnap victims, so I was expecting to get a good night's sleep. Of course, a good night's sleep turned out to be the exact opposite of the night ahead of me.

Chapter 9

The dream started with a long walk down a dark hallway. I had no idea where the hallway might be located and suspected that it wasn't actually real. The passage was too dark and too long to be an actual place. I wasn't sure how I knew that my dream tonight would be different, but as the man walked down the hallway and I became aware of my surroundings, my heart began to race. While I was still asleep, I was also aware. I knew my heart was racing as the journey continued, and my fear intensified.

"I was wondering when you'd show up," the man I was channeling said to me telepathically.

"It's so dark. Where are we?" I asked.

"That is not a detail you need to know at this point." He opened a door and turned a light on. The glare was blinding after the dark. I could feel my pulse quicken even more as the man's eyes adjusted to the light, and I was able to make out the images in the room.

"Shredder!" I exclaimed as the man focused on a man who was lying on the cement floor. "Is he alive?"

"Yes, he's alive. At least for now. I'm afraid I might have given him too much of the drug I used to subdue him, however. He hasn't regained consciousness, but he should be fine once he does."

I wanted to scream, but I wasn't actually in control of my body. "Are you going to kill him?" I asked in my dream.

"Eventually. You have a few days to try to rescue him."

I couldn't see the man's face, but I could tell that he was amused by the whole thing.

"You say that he's alive now, but I'm not sure I believe you. I'd like to check him out for myself. Just so I can know that he actually is alive. Will you get closer?"

"I'd like to comply, but I think it's time for you to wake up."

With that, I woke up. I took a moment to get my bearings, and then I slowly sat up. I was sitting in the bed, and the dogs were all looking at me. I suspect I might actually have managed a scream after all.

"I need to call Houston," I said. I slipped out of bed and dialed his number, hoping he'd answer despite the late hour.

"Harmony?" he asked after the second ring.

"It's Shredder. The man who I've been channeling has him. Please, you have to help me figure out what to do."

"Hang tight. I'm on my way."

I decided to go ahead and get dressed, and then I began brewing a pot of coffee. When Houston arrived, I filled him in on my dream and asked what he thought we should do.

"You've tried calling Shredder?" Houston asked.

"Numerous times. I'm really scared. I have no idea who Shredder works for, but I feel like we should notify someone," I said. "Maybe the CIA."

"Have you tried to connect with Shredder directly?" Houston asked.

"No. I didn't know Shredder was in trouble until I had the dream. I guess the man who has him must have taken him after we left to respond to the kidnapped child." Suddenly I realized that the kidnapped child might have been nothing more than a diversion to get Houston and me out of the way. But why involve us at all? If Shredder was on this man's list, why not grab him after he left Rescue. During the dream, I had the feeling that the man was waiting for me to show up. It almost felt like he'd taken Shredder just to get to me. But why? I swallowed my terror. "We need to find him."

"I know he was unconscious in the dream, but I really do think that at this point, trying to connect is our best bet. Something very high level is going on. Chances are that the person behind this is highly trained and is most likely a member of a group similar to the one that employs Shredder. I'm not sure it's a good idea to bring anyone else into things until we know more about what we're dealing with."

I decided that Houston was right, so I agreed to try to connect. I sat down on the sofa and pictured Shredder's crooked smile and bright blue eyes. I pictured his bleached blond hair and surfer-boy tan. I tried harder than I ever had to make a connection, but nothing was coming to me. I knew that Shredder would let me in if he could feel my presence, which meant that he was likely still unconscious.

Tears streamed down my face as I continued to try.

"Take a break, Harm," Houston said.

"I can't get through to him."

"Take a break, and we'll try again in an hour. We'll keep trying for as long as it takes."

"Okay." I agreed. I supposed wearing myself out when Shredder was likely still unconscious wasn't the best idea.

"How's your head?" Houston asked.

"It feels like it might explode at any minute, but that's okay. I'm going to take a break as you suggested, and then I'm going to keep going. I need to keep going."

"Why don't you find Moose, and I'll grab you some aspirin. I agree that we may need to eventually call someone, but as we discussed, I hate to make things worse by calling the wrong person. I don't suppose Shredder has ever mentioned a contact."

"No, he's never indicated who I should call if he was in trouble. I'm going to try to close my eyes and rest for a few minutes and then try again. If I can get through, then not only can he tell us where he is, but he can tell us who to call for help."

Houston's suggestion to grab Moose was a good one. Moose was my emotional therapy cat who seemed to lessen the pain I took on when I allowed my mind to connect with another. There were times when I wasn't sure how I would have done what needed to be done if not for the comfort the furry Maine Coon brought me.

I cringed as a sharp pain shot through my head. After settling in with Moose, I closed my eyes and tried to relax. I knew that connecting with Shredder sooner rather than later was going to be imperative if Shredder was still alive and saving him was a viable option, but the pain in my head was so immense that there was no way I was going to be able to connect with anyone until I got it under control.

"Denali is throwing a fit to go out," Houston said. "I'll take all the dogs for a quick walk while you rest."

"Okay," I agreed. That really did seem to be the best idea at this point.

After about twenty minutes, Houston walked in through the front door with a cell phone in his hand. "How are you feeling?" he asked.

"Better. Thanks. What do you have there?"

He held it up. "A cell phone. I'm going to assume that it belongs to Shredder."

I nodded. "I think so. Shredder had a cell phone and was waiting for a call when I had to leave for the rescue. The man who has him must have snuck up on him while he was outside."

"I guess that explains how the kidnapper got past the dogs."

"I guess it does. Denali would have eaten the kidnapper alive if he could have gotten to him. Can you access the phone?"

Houston tried. "It's locked. I guess that's to be expected."

"Maybe Landon can do something with it," I said hopefully. Landon wasn't a professional hacker like Shredder, but he did seem to know his way around electronic equipment.

"I'll call him and ask him to come by," Houston suggested.

I closed my eyes and tried to connect with Shredder once again. I sort of doubted that the kidnapper had taken the unconscious man too far, so my hope was that he was still in Alaska.

"Any luck?" Houston asked after I opened my eyes.

I blew out a breath. "No. I'm not sure I'll be able to connect with Shredder even when he regains consciousness. It doesn't always work."

"I know, but we'll keep trying."

"I just don't understand why the man who has Shredder is doing what he's doing. We know he kidnapped three individuals who all worked in the intelligence industry. We know that at least one of the three kidnap victims is dead, and we know that the man who kidnapped these three individuals kept them for at least two weeks. Why? And why was he just sitting there in the room waiting for me to connect with him? He didn't seem surprised to feel my presence. In fact, he said something about wondering when I'd show up. The whole thing is not only very disturbing, but it really makes no sense."

"I agree with you. I've been trying to figure out what this man's end game is, but to tell you the truth, I'm as confused as you are. I'm sure that if I was the one on the run with someone like Shredder, every instinct I possess would be telling me to get as far away from Rescue as I could. If this guy is simply holed up somewhere in the area, there must be something more going on than meets the eye."

Houston and I sat quietly for a moment before either of us spoke.

"I think I'm ready to try again," I said.

"It's only been thirty minutes."

"I know, but I want to try to connect with Shredder as soon as he wakes up, so I need to keep trying."

Houston blew out a breath. "Okay. How can I support you?"

"Just hold my hand."

Houston did as I asked, and I closed my eyes and focused. It still hadn't worked by the time Landon showed up, so I took a break. Landon looked at the phone and assured us that he'd try to get in, but that without the password, he doubted he'd be successful with a security system as sophisticated as the one installed on Shredder's cell phone.

"Just keep trying," I said before taking my cat and heading to the bedroom to try to connect once again. It took several more tries, but eventually, I connected with a very groggy Shredder.

"Shredder, is that you?" I anxiously asked.

"Harmony?"

"Shhh. Don't say anything. I'm in your head. Just think about what you want to say, and I'll be able to hear you."

"There's someone at the door."

With that, he was gone.

"What happened?" Houston asked after he came into the bedroom to find me propped up on a stack of pillows.

"I was able to connect with Shredder, but only for a moment."

"Is he okay?"

"He sounded okay. Groggy but alert. I was only able to maintain the connection for a few seconds, and then someone came in."

"I guess you can try again later."

I put my hands on my head. "Yeah, I will."

"Maybe you should get some sleep," Houston said. "I'll stay here," he added. "I'll take the dogs out while you at least lay down and close your eyes."

"Okay," I agreed, reluctant to go along with the plan but understanding that I really did need to maintain my strength.

Chapter 10

I guess the long night of trying to connect with Shredder must have taken more out of me than I realized. My intention was to close my eyes for just a few minutes, but when I next woke, five hours had passed. Landon was gone, but Houston assured me that he'd taken the phone with him and would continue to try to get past the extensive security.

"Why'd you let me sleep so long?" I asked Houston once I realized how much time had passed.

"You were exhausted and needed to recharge, and chances are that Shredder needed time to get his bearings as well. Did you dream about the kidnapper?"

"No." I ran a hand through my hair. "I don't remember dreaming at all. I'm going to take a shower and then have something to eat so that I'm fully alert. After that, I'm going to try connecting with Shredder again."

"I think that sounds like a good idea. I called my office to let them know I was working on a lead relating to the man we found in the cabin but would come in if they needed me. Once you've had a chance to shower and eat, you and I will sit down and come up with a strategy."

Given the fact that I'd been able to briefly connect with Shredder before we were interrupted, I assumed I'd be able to reconnect once I had the opportunity to try again, but after hours of failed attempts, I had begun to suspect that Shredder might be dead. I knew that if I was going to find my friend, dead or alive, I needed to stay focused and try not to panic, but keeping my calm in this situation was turning out to be one of the hardest things I'd ever had to do.

"Okay, let's evaluate where we are," Houston said after it became apparent that reconnecting with Shredder wasn't going to be as easy as we hoped. "We know that when you connected with him earlier, Shredder was alive. We know he's being held by the same man who kidnapped the other three intelligence operatives, and we know that in the other three cases, the kidnapper waited at least two weeks before severing his relationship with these individuals. We know that the third kidnap victim we're aware of was killed and left in a cabin here in Alaska. We don't know with any degree of certainty the fate of the other two kidnap victims, but at this point, we're assuming that they are dead."

"All of that sounds right," I said.

"This man seems to know you are lurking around in his head, and, based on what you've said, he seems intrigued by the whole thing. Amused even. In my mind, it's possible that this man took Shredder, who he probably observed spending time with you, as a means of goading you into upping your game. While Shredder is in intelligence, and he may have been the next victim all along, it almost feels like his kidnapping had more to do with you than him."

I supposed Houston had a point. Shredder seemed to think the first three victims taken by this man were linked to one another in some way. He'd shared that it was his opinion that the man seemed to have some sort of list he was using to choose his victims. If that was the case, then the question was whether or not Shredder was on that initial list. If he wasn't, then maybe Houston was right, and my friend had become a victim because of me and for no other reason.

"Okay, so how do we find him?" I asked.

Houston paused. "What do you remember from your connection with the kidnapper and from your brief connection with Shredder last night?"

"During my dream that first night, the man seemed to be sitting in a chair. He said he'd been waiting for me. He seemed to have a basic understanding of the way this whole thing works. He turned his head so that I could see that he had Shredder even though Shredder was unconscious. He assured me that my friend was okay but that he must have given him too much of some sort of sedative."

"And what did the room look like? Was the kidnapper holding Shredder in a house? A shed? A garage? Warehouse?"

I took a deep breath and tried to remember. "There were metal shelves lined along bare walls. The floor was concrete. Shredder was handcuffed to one of the frames supporting the metal shelves. I'm going to say the enclosure was a garage or warehouse of some sort. I could only see what the man I was channeling allowed me to see. Unfortunately, that wasn't a lot."

"Close your eyes and try to remember exactly what you saw. You said that Shredder was handcuffed to the frame of one of the shelves that lined the walls. Was he sitting in a chair? On the floor?"

"He was lying on the floor."

"Was there anything on the shelf he was handcuffed to?"

I frowned. "I'm not sure. I was focused on Shredder and not on the items on the shelves."

Houston took my hand and gave it a squeeze. "Just try to think back. You're in your dream, and you connect with the kidnapper. You can see what he can see, and he allows you to see Shredder. Shredder is handcuffed to shelving that has been placed along each wall. You can see that he's unconscious. The kidnapper knows you're in his head, and he assures you that Shredder is alive for now. The kidnapper keeps his distance even when you ask for a closer look. The shelves behind Shredder must be visible through the kidnapper's eyes. What do you see?"

I focused in to the best of my ability. It wasn't easy since I really hadn't been focused in on anything other than Shredder. Eventually, I noticed that there had been items on the shelves in the room where Shredder was. "Crab traps. There are crab traps on the shelves." I opened my eyes. "Crabs are harvested in the winter, so the traps must be in storage."

"So the room where Shredder is being held must be near the sea. Maybe Valdez or Homer. Possibly even south of there. The facility is likely a warehouse of some sort, but there are so many possible locations. We'll need more."

I leaned my head back and suppressed a groan. There were simply too many possible locations to be able to take our search for Shredder on the road.

"Should we call someone?" I asked.

Houston hesitated. "It feels like we should, but who? We don't know who Shredder works for or who knows about him. I'd hate to mess things up for him if he has this under control. If you're able to connect with him again, at the very least, we can ask him what he wants us to do."

"So I should keep trying."

Houston nodded. "For now. I guess if we can't make contact or figure out a physical location to search, we'll have no option but to call someone. Maybe the CIA."

I got up and stretched my arms over my head. "Okay. I'm going to take the dogs for a walk and try to clear my head. When I get back, I'll try again. If I'm unsuccessful, I guess I'll just try to sleep. If I can't make a connection with Shredder, maybe I can connect with the kidnapper again."

"Do you think it's likely that you will?" Houston asked.

I shrugged. "I don't know. In the past, I've only dreamt of this man every few nights. I'm not sure if he has to let me in or if I need to be in a specific dream state to make the connection. I'm honestly not sure how it works when I'm asleep. I have a much better understanding of how things work when I'm awake and alert and have the intention to connect. I feel like connecting with Shredder is our best bet, so that's where I'm going to focus my energy."

I got up and headed into my bedroom for my shoes. When I returned, Houston was waiting for me. Kojak had joined my pack near the door. It seemed that based on our movements, they'd all realized that a walk was in their future.

"I'll need to check on the animals in the barn when we get back," I said to Houston after grabbing my rifle and heading out the door.

"I can take care of them if you'd like."

"Actually, I don't mind. Feeding the animals and cleaning Homer's stall is oddly calming. Maybe it's the routine or the fresh smell of new hay. I'm not exactly sure why, but I do find that caring for my 'kids' brings me a lot of satisfaction."

"I get it. I enjoy brushing Kojak, and that dog needs a lot of brushing." He laughed. "I have no idea how you keep all your dogs groomed."

"The spring shed can be tough, but otherwise, the dogs do okay with weekly brushings, so I just rotate who gets a comb out each evening." When we arrived at the lake, I settled on a log that had fallen near the lakeshore during a winter storm. I wasn't sure what was going to happen next, but if I was able to connect with Shredder and narrow in on his location, there was a good chance that Houston and I would take to the road and leave the dogs with Serena. Serena was great with the animals, and they enjoyed spending time with her, but she didn't have time to take them on long walks every day. I figured I'd let them swim now in the event they had to go a few days with short walks around my property.

"I wonder if it would be worth our time to try to figure out why the first three victims were taken," Houston said. "Shredder thought the three were related in some way. If we can figure out how they're related, we might be able to determine whether Shredder would have been on the initial list or if he was taken because of the relationship you seem to have stumbled into with the kidnapper."

"How are we going to figure that out?" I asked. "It's not like the sorts of things these specific individuals did would end up in the newspaper or on the internet."

"True," Houston admitted. "I suppose if we can get through to Shredder, he might know."

I stood up. "I think I'm ready to head back. I feel this urgency to figure out if Shredder is alive, and the only way I can do that is to make a connection. I have to keep trying."

Houston took my hand. We didn't say a word about the fact that he was holding my hand as we walked back toward my cabin, but it was warm and comforting. It was nice to know I wasn't in this alone.

Houston offered once again to take care of the animals in the barn when we returned to the cabin, and this time I decided to let him. I gathered Moose up in my arms, sat down on the sofa, closed my eyes, and focused. I let myself experience Shredder's sweet smile and his surfer-boy looks. I tried to create a photo in my mind to cling to.

"Hello there, yellow sweater," a voice said in my mind.

Okay, not the person I was going for, but maybe this would do. "The man you are holding. Is he okay?"

"For now."

"Can I see him?"

"I suppose that can be arranged. But I'm not going to risk one of these mind melds. I'm keeping your man drugged up. If you want to see the man conscious one more time before I kill him, you'll need to find him."

It was apparent to me that this man seemed to think this whole thing was one big game. I wanted to ask him why on earth he thought I'd walk into a trap, but even as I had the thought, I knew that was exactly what I was going to do. "Where are you?"

"Too easy. You need to find us."

"Can I have a clue?"

"Alaska. We're still in Alaska."

That actually was helpful.

"Here are the rules," the man continued. "Really, there is just one rule. No cops. No FBI, CIA, MI6, Interpol, or anyone else. If you want to see your friend again, you come alone."

"Okay," I agreed, knowing that Houston would never go for it but figuring that we'd work out a plan once the connection was broken. "I'll come alone. How much time do I have?"

I hoped the man would answer, but he didn't before the connection was broken.

Moose was squirming to get down by this point, so I let him go. I guessed I had been squeezing him harder than usual. I'd only been connected with the man for a few minutes, so I figured Houston was still in the barn. I decided to take a minute to try to remember what I'd seen. Shredder was definitely being held in a warehouse of some sort. I remembered the crab traps that I'd seen through the kidnapper's eyes, and this time I noticed a sign within the line of sight of the man I was channeling. The sign was partially blocked by a stack of boxes, but I noticed a crab with a crown in the upper left-hand corner of the sign. Maybe a logo? I got up and grabbed my computer. I looked for crabbing operations with a logo that included a crab with a crown. King Leopold Charters advertised halibut, salmon, shrimp, and crab, and their logo was a crab with a crown. According to their website, in addition to having offices in Anchorage, they had boats running from Seward, Homer, Ketchikan, and Juno. Chances are the gear would be stored near each operation, so I supposed that Shredder could be found in any of these five locations.

"Any luck?" Houston asked after he walked in through the front door with the dogs.

"Yes and no."

"Care to elaborate?"

"I tried to connect with Shredder but was unsuccessful. I was, however, able to connect with the man who took Shredder. I still don't know who he is or where he is, but he did say that Shredder was still alive."

Houston blew out a breath. "I guess that's something. Maybe you'll be able to connect with Shredder later."

I tucked my feet up under my body. "I doubt it, although I do plan to try. The man I connected with knew I was there. He seemed to be expecting me. He told me that he has Shredder drugged up so that I can't connect with him. I think this guy somehow knows how this all works and has taken my ability to connect with Shredder to provide clues off the table."

"So what exactly is this guy's plan?" Houston asked.

"I think he wants to play a game with me. He told me I had to find Shredder if I wanted to see him alive again before he killed him. He told me that it was up to me to follow the clues to find them, but really all he told me was that he was still in Alaska. Alaska is a big state, so that isn't much of a clue, but while I was chatting with this guy, I happened to notice a sign for King Leopold Charters. King Leopold Charters has an office in Anchorage. They also have boats running from Seward, Homer, Ketchikan, and Juno. I think the best place to start is these five locations. I'm not sure which would be a better guess than the others, so I may have to check them all out."

Houston sat down next to me. "I need to make some calls, but I guess we should get going."

"Yeah, about that. The guy said no cops, and he said to come alone."

Houston's face tightened. "There's no way you're going alone."

"I know. And trust me, I don't want to. This whole thing is obviously a trap of some sort. But this guy is probably watching, so I can't go charging in with the cavalry either. I've been thinking about it, and I think we should begin our search in Anchorage. We'll fly down separately. Maybe even separate flights. There are several flights a day between Fairbanks and Anchorage. We can stay in adjoining rooms at the same hotel. That way, we can work together without leaving a paper trail announcing that we're traveling together. I'll rent a car, and you can rent your own car or take a cab to the hotel. Once we get there, we'll figure it out."

Houston hesitated. I wasn't sure what I was going to do if he rejected my plan, but in the end, he agreed to at least follow my plan to the point I'd outlined it. He needed to pack and arrange things at work. I needed to call Serena and ask her to stay at my place and take care of the animals. She'd done that in the past and didn't seem to mind. There was a flight in three hours and another in seven. I bought a ticket for the flight in three hours, and Houston bought a ticket for the flight in seven. I called and reserved a room at a hotel near the airport, and then Houston called and asked for an adjoining room. It would be late by the time he arrived, so he'd also arranged for a late check-in and the ability to use an app on his cell phone as the room key. I knew I'd need to hurry to make my flight, so I called Serena, who was just getting off for the day, and she agreed to come right over. I packed while I waited for her. Once she arrived, I went over everything I needed her to take care of and headed to the airport. I was really going to have to hustle to make my flight. I knew I needed to call Jake, but he was going to have a huge problem with this whole thing, so I figured I'd just call him after I arrived at the hotel.

I literally had to run through the airport to make my flight. I supposed that trying to pack, drive to Fairbanks, and check-in all within three hours was a crazy idea in the first place, but now that I had a plan, I was anxious to get started. When I arrived in Anchorage, the line at the car rental place was crazy long, so by the time I got my car, drove to the hotel, and checked in, Houston was likely already in the air. I was starving, so I called room service and ordered a club sandwich and a side of fries. I figured I'd eat and then call Jake. He'd likely be at Neverland tonight, so maybe it would be busy, and he wouldn't have time to throw too much of a fit. I was happy that I had tonight off. If I'd been expected at work. I would have had to call in before I left, and big brother Jake would have certainly tried to stop me.

"Hey, Serena." I decided to call and check in with Serena first. I knew I was stalling, but I also knew Jake would be upset that I'd taken off on this game of cat and mouse without talking to him about it first.

"I take it you made it to the hotel okay."

"I did." I hadn't told Serena the whole story. She didn't know a thing about Shredder or his top-secret life, so it would have been hard to explain things even if I'd wanted to. I simply told her Houston needed my help on a case and that I'd be gone for up to a week. She assured me that she was happy to stay at my place and keep an eye on the animals. I'd offered to let Kojak stay with Serena and my crew, but Houston had decided to drop him off with Harley and Brando. "It's actually a really nice room."

"Nice and romantic?" Serena teased.

I laughed. Serena had tried more than once to get Houston and me together in a way that was different than our current friendship. "No. Just nice. Houston and I are working. We have separate rooms. This isn't a romantic getaway."

"Too bad. A week together on a case seems the perfect time to explore options in other areas."

If not for the fact that I was terrified that I'd never see Shredder alive again, I might have agreed with Serena's statement. Deciding that the easiest way to get Serena off this line of questioning was to change the subject, I asked her about the animals and then reminded her about the supplements the older dogs took each day.

"Harley was in today," Serena informed me after I'd exhausted the subject of supplements.

"Did he come in alone, or was Brittany with him?"

"He was alone. He said that Brittany decided to head to Anchorage to do some shopping, so he was on his own for a few days. He decided to put in some volunteer hours while Brando hung out with the dogs. He ended up staying right up until he got a call from Houston asking him to keep Kojak for him while he was away."

"I guess the fact that Brittany is in Anchorage shopping and not in Harley's house doing things of an intimate nature should prove to you that Harley and Brittany really are just friends."

"Maybe." She paused. "I hope so."

We chatted for a few minutes, and then I hung up and called Jake. As expected, he was less than thrilled that I was in Anchorage looking for Shredder.

"This sounds like a trap," he pointed out.

"I'm sure it is, but I can't just let Shredder die. Houston is on his way down. Once he gets here, we'll come up with a plan that will allow us to save Shredder without getting ourselves killed."

"Maybe I should come down," Jake insisted.

"No. Not yet. The guy said to come alone. I've gone to a lot of trouble to appear to be alone if anyone is watching. I need to do this. Shredder is my friend. We all owe him a lot."

He sighed. "Yeah, I know. But I'm worried about you."

"I'll be careful. And I'll call you every day."

"More than once a day. At least twice. Call me in the morning to fill me in on the plan you and Houston come up with tonight and call me tomorrow night after you return to the hotel and let me know how things went."

"Okay," I agreed. "I'll keep you in the loop. But remember that no one else can know about this. Tell Landon to keep quiet about what he knows as well. If anyone asks where I am, make something up. Maybe you can say I'm in search and rescue training or that you sent me to check out a potential S&R dog."

"Okay. I'll figure something out. And Harm, be careful."

"Always."

By the time I hung up, I had just enough time to take a shower and freshen up a bit before Houston arrived. My energy was beginning to fade, and I wanted to be alert and helpful once Houston arrived. I really had no idea how we were going to save

Shredder once we found him, but at this point, I just assumed we'd take things one step at a time.

Chapter 11

I actually had a bit more energy once Houston arrived. As we planned, he checked into the room next to mine and then joined me in my room via the adjoining door. Unless our kidnapper had cameras in the room, which I sincerely doubted, there would be no way for him to know that Houston was with me.

"I bought us each a burner phone," Houston said, handing mine to me. "Based on the fact that this guy has kidnapped and killed so many very qualified assets, I'm going to assume he has the ability to hack into our phones, emails, computers, and anything else he sees fit. My plan is to leave our computers and my cell phone in the rooms when we head out. We'll use the burner phones to communicate with each other. As for your personal cell phone, I think it might prove useful as a decoy."

"So I take my cell phone somewhere like the library, where I stash it while we're checking out the warehouse."

"Something like that. We need to assume that this man knows you're in Anchorage. It would be easy enough to get your flight information, as well as information relating to your rental car and the hotel you've chosen to stay in. Knowing that he most likely has all this information will actually help us."

"I like the way you're thinking. Go on."

Houston pulled a map out. "I realize that paper maps are almost obsolete, but since we want to keep our thoughts to ourselves, I thought it best not to use an internet map or search engine."

"I agree. What are those areas on the map marked in red?"

"Properties in Anchorage associated with or owned by King Leopold Charters. This here," he said as he pointed to an area in the middle of town, "is the corporate offices. It's unlikely that our kidnapper is holding Shredder there. Even if the kidnapper is associated with King Leopold Charters in some way, which I honestly doubt, I think it highly unlikely that he'd be holding a captive in such a public place."

"I agree."

Houston pointed to another building not all that far away from the headquarters. "This is a shop of sorts. Repairs to the fishing equipment are taken care of here. There may be storage rooms in this building as well, but the place looks to be populated with workers year-round, so, again, I doubt Shredder is being held there."

"I agree with that as well."

"This," Houston said as he pointed to an area that he'd marked on the water in Seward, "is where the boat that is run out of Seward is docked. Initially, I considered the idea that this man was holding Shredder on a boat, but this particular charter boat is popular and often booked, so I doubt anyone is being held there."

It seemed that would be true of any of the boats or warehouses. What we needed was a location the company no longer used. Perhaps a warehouse where they stored seasonal or outdated equipment. Houston must have had a similar thought since he pointed to another location marked in red. This one was not on the water, but it was close enough to the dock that it was feasible that it might be used for storage.

"I think, in terms of finding a location in either Anchorage or Seward that could potentially be used to hide a kidnap victim, this location is our best bet. I honestly don't expect to find Shredder in Seward since there are other locations that make more sense, but I think it would be a mistake to discount a possible holding area without checking it out."

"I agree. Should we head to Seward tomorrow?"

Houston didn't answer right away. I could see that he was thinking things over. This was a complicated situation that would have benefited from Shredder's assistance. It really was too bad the man who had him was keeping him drugged up.

"At this point, the kidnapper doesn't know that you noticed the King Leopold sign. Or at least I guess we can assume he doesn't know that you stumbled onto that clue. If the guy is really good, he may have fed it to you, but for now, let's assume that he doesn't know that you know about the link between a King Leopold facility and the location where he's holed up. I think it would be a mistake to go straight to this location. If he is watching, we need to mix things up a bit."

"Okay. How?" I asked.

"It would be helpful to talk to someone in the corporate office about the various locations where the company does business or stores supplies. I have a buddy who can hook me up with what I need to fake being a Department of Health and Safety official. I thought this through during the flight south, and it seems to make the most sense to me that I go in under the guise of a surprise audit while you follow another lead. A fake lead that is in no way associated with King Leopold Charters."

"That way, the kidnapper won't know what we know."

"Exactly."

"But we are going to go after Shredder, right? I mean, that is the point of the whole thing."

"We are. My idea is to have you run around town chasing your tail while I get a look inside the headquarters. We'll regroup at the hotel, and once we look at the maps I plan to ask for from the folks at King Leopold Charters, we can leave your cell phone at the hotel and then head to Seward. We'll take my rental car since the kidnapper might be watching yours. I'm hoping the folks at the corporate office will be able to tell me which buildings or facilities associated with their enterprise are currently staffed and which are used for storage only."

I had to admit that Houston had a good plan. I was somewhat skeptical that he'd be able to pull off his role without being noticed. He, however, was confident and assured me that with the proper uniform and identification, no one would question what he was doing. I just hoped he was right.

Once we decided on this plan, Houston made a call. It sounded like whoever he was talking to had fake IDs and uniforms just sitting around and available for use. I wasn't sure what to make of that but decided not to ask. Houston arranged to pick the items he'd requested up the following morning. Once he had that arranged, we went to work setting up a series of stops for me to make. If they were too bogus, the man who was likely watching me would catch on. Still, I didn't want him to know I knew about the King Leopold link, so Houston and I discussed places I might search had I not known what I did. I supposed if I didn't know which warehouse to search, I'd still search warehouses since even the kidnapper must have realized I'd seen enough of the background to figure that much out. Houston helped me identify some likely candidates well away from the area where he planned to spend the day. Once we had our plan, Houston went back to his room. I knew what I needed to do, and he had a plan for the day, so we decided it would be best if we didn't meet the following morning unless one of us felt it was important. I had my burner phone, which could be used to contact Houston if needed. He reminded me to bring both phones with me when I went out tomorrow for day one of my search for Shredder. I found myself wishing I was going to be the one to go to the headquarters since that seemed a more active role to take, but I knew Houston's plan made sense, so I decided to heed his expertise and do things his way.

Chapter 12

When I woke the following morning dream-free, I wasn't sure whether to be happy that I'd gotten a good night's rest or worried that I hadn't connected with the kidnapper. Not that this man and I had connected every night. Far from it. The connections had been sparse in the beginning but had become more frequent now that the man realized I was in his head. I wondered when exactly he'd first noticed me lurking around in there. He seemed amused by the whole thing at this point, but I had to wonder what his initial reaction had been.

It was early. Barely five a.m. I decided to try to connect with Shredder one more time. I knew the man had drugged him in order to prevent me from having access to his mind, but since I hadn't dreamt about the man last night, that might indicate that he'd slept, and if he had, he might not have given Shredder a new dose of the knockout drug this morning.

I didn't have Moose or Houston or anyone to use as an anchor, so I braced myself for whatever sort of head-piercing pain I might experience as I tried to find my way to my friend. If I didn't connect right away, I'd stop. No use wearing myself out before the day even began. I closed my eyes, imagined Shredder's face, and concentrated as hard as I could.

"Harmony?"

I wanted to cry with relief. "Yes. It's me. I'm in Anchorage with Houston. We're here to rescue you. I don't suppose you happen to know where you are."

He looked around the small room he was locked in. It was completely barren and free of windows. "I'm not sure. I've been moved. I was in a warehouse with fishing and crabbing supplies, but all I can see are bare walls at this point."

"We need to narrow this down. The kidnapper knows I'm in his head. He's been communicating with me. He's given me a limited amount of time to find you, although I'm not clear how long that is. I suspect that if I don't find you in that time, he will kill you."

"That's good to know." He paused and then continued. "There's something you need to know, and I don't know how much time I'll have, so listen closely."

"Okay."

"First off, I'm fine, and I'm touched that you are here to save me, but I don't want to be saved just yet, so take your time tracking me down."

"What? Why should I take my time?"

"I need more time, and while a rescue would be great, I'd prefer to be rescued toward the end of the time you were given."

"You've totally lost your mind."

"Not at all. This man has killed at least three people, and, as far as I can tell, there are others on his list. I need to find out what his plans are and how to stop him."

"You allowed yourself to be kidnapped," I realized. I was going to wring the man's neck as soon as I rescued him. Talk about a reckless risk.

I couldn't see his face, but I was sure he smiled at this point. "I had a plan. A plan that went awry when the man who kidnapped me realized I had a tracking device implanted under my skin and cut it out."

"Tracking device?"

"Everyone in my organization has one so the others can find us. It's not important at this point. My team will be looking for me in the last place I was physically located before the tracker was cut out. I assume the tracker was left behind as a decoy. I'm not sure where the tracker might be at this point since it was cut out after I was drugged and taken hostage, but I suspect it may have been wherever the warehouse where you first connected with me is located."

"Should I contact someone?"

"Not yet. The members of the team I work with aren't the sort who believe in psychics. Given the information you possess, they're never going to believe that you aren't involved with the kidnapper. In fact, rather than listening to what you have to say, they'd likely detain you. At this point, I think you are my best chance of being found, and for now, I think the two of us should work together. I'll let you know if I can think of a way for you to share information with my team without putting yourself in the middle of this."

My head was pounding by this point, and I wasn't even sure I'd be able to maintain the connection, but I had to try. "Okay. What do you want me to do?"

"Tell me what you know."

I explained about King Leopold Charters, the sign I'd seen through the kidnapper's eyes, and the plan Houston and I had come up with. Shredder agreed that our plan made sense. Shredder shared that while he couldn't see anything in the dark room that he'd been locked up in, he could hear noises coming from beyond his cell that could best be attributed to a location on or near a dock. He said he smelled salt and dead fish, and he could hear seagulls and boat engines. Shredder also said that the kidnapper seemed to be staying longer to chat with him when he brought his food and water and that he hoped this would allow him to begin a conversation that would lead to the answers he was after.

"Do you really think he'll tell you his plan?" I asked.

"Why not. The man plans to kill me anyway. If he gets bored enough, I might be able to get him to talk."

"I really hate this idea. What if I can't find you in time?"

"You will. If you can connect with the kidnapper, do so, but don't mention or let on that we have connected as well. It's going to give us the upper hand if the man believes I'm totally helpless."

"You are helpless."

"Actually, I'm not. I need to go. I hear movement from the other side of the door. Try connecting with me later. Maybe after you return from your errands today."

With that, he was gone.

I could tell this was going to be a frustrating investigation. I wanted Shredder safe and out of the hands of this killer now, but while he seemed to want me to find him, he wanted me to wait to rescue him. In my mind, that was asking a lot. I glanced at the clock and decided to head for the shower. Houston and I had agreed not to meet this morning, so I decided to keep with that plan and head out to search the warehouses that the two of us had identified. I was to meet him back in the rooms later this afternoon, and I supposed that was soon enough to fill him in.

Chapter 13

After my conversation with Shredder, I felt even more determined to figure out exactly where the man who had taken him captive was holding him. The kidnapper had said I had limited time to find him, but I didn't know how long. I supposed if I had the opportunity to chat with him again, I'd ask him that very question. I'd hate to be late to the rescue simply because the two of us were on different timelines. Of course, I still had to find Shredder. He said he thought he was being held near a dock or marina. This was coastal Alaska, so that really didn't narrow things down much.

The warehouses Houston and I had decided on for today's search were either deserted or used for seasonal storage. We knew it was unlikely that the kidnapper would be holding Shredder in a location populated by people, and we knew that the kidnapper would know that I'd realized that as well. Even though I knew that the locations we'd selected for today's search were unlikely to lead to a rescue, I couldn't prevent my heart from pounding each time I approached one of the large buildings. I wasn't sure if the kidnapper was tracking my movements, but I made sure that I had my cell phone with me at all times in case he was using it to watch my progress.

It was while I was walking around the fifth warehouse I'd been assigned to check out, looking in windows and searching buildings not even considered to be contenders, that I received a text. The text had been sent from an unknown source and simply contained a GPS location. The location was nowhere near any of the buildings Houston and I had agreed that I'd check out today, but I couldn't ignore what appeared to be a clue or perhaps instructions of some sort. I knew that Houston wouldn't be happy if I strayed from the plan we'd agreed upon, but I didn't feel right simply ignoring the text.

I considered calling Houston using the burner phone he'd given me, but he'd only instruct me to ignore the text, so, making a decision, I headed back to my rental car and followed the map leading to the location I'd been given.

"Can I help you, Miss?" a weathered old sea captain asked after I arrived at the GPS location only to find a rusty old boat tied to a crumbling dock.

I looked around for a building or warehouse where someone might be held captive, but all I could see were boats. "I'm not sure. I was sent to this location by a friend. I thought I was to meet someone, but apparently, I got things wrong." I considered my next move before continuing. "I don't suppose you've seen a man around here in the past few days. Tall. Blond. Tanned."

The man paused to think about things. "No. I can't say that I have. Sounds like the sort of fella you'd find in Hawaii, not Alaska."

"Yes. My friend does look like he's spent time in a tropical location. He's just visiting the area."

"Sorry, Miss. I haven't seen anyone looking like that."

I thanked the man and was preparing to leave when I noticed that the man's boat was actually identified as The Sea Witch of Homer, Alaska. "Are you normally based in Homer?" I asked.

"Yup. In the area for some repairs. Need to take on a couple of crew as well. Already been here ten days and need to get back, but hoped to get that taken care of before heading out. I don't suppose you know anyone who is looking for work."

"No. I'm sorry. I'm a visitor to the area, so I don't know anyone." I looked around and tried to determine if there was a clue that I was missing. I supposed the clue could be Homer, or the clue could be The Sea Witch. I had no idea how a vessel that was based out of Homer but was docked in Anchorage might play into this game I seem to have been drawn into, but if the kidnapper was actually helping me, then I supposed I should be grateful that he seemed to have a reason to want me to succeed.

After returning to my car, I just sat there for a few minutes. There were two more buildings on my original list, but at this point, searching them seemed pointless. If, in fact, it had been the kidnapper who had sent me the GPS location, which in my mind was the only person who could have sent it, then the clue I was meant to find had to have been there and not in any of the other locations we'd identified.

Once I returned to the hotel, I searched for The Sea Witch of Homer, Alaska, on my computer. If the kidnapper had sent me the clue, then he knew I had it and would expect me to follow up. If I'd stumbled across the clue in some other way, I would have avoided doing an internet search from my personal account.

My search netted me the information that The Sea Witch was registered at the City of Homer Port and Harbor. I jotted down the slip number where it was usually kept and then pulled up a map of the area. The Sea Witch was a midsized boat that would require a larger slip with deep-water access. The slip assigned was accessible via a series of ladders and walkways. I wasn't sure why I'd been provided this clue or even if the clue I'd been provided was a legitimate lead. For all I knew, the kidnapper wanted to distract me from my investigation this afternoon and had sent me off in the wrong direction, but Homer was on our list of places where King Leopold operated out of, so perhaps Houston and I should head there next rather than wasting time in Seward.

"Okay, Harm," I said aloud to myself. "What's going on here? Is The Sea Witch a clue? A distraction? What about Homer as a location? Clue or distraction?" I thought about what I'd seen when I'd followed the directions provided to me. "I suppose the clue might have been something other than the boat. Would I even have homed in on that specific vessel if the captain hadn't been there? There were other boats docked in the area." I closed my eyes and groaned. I really didn't know what to do at this point. Houston and I had come up with a plan that included our heading to Seward tonight. Should we stick with our plan or pack up, check out, and head to Homer? I hated to waste even a single hour since I really had no idea when my clock had begun or how long I had to find Shredder. Still, I didn't want to get lured in by a fake clue or faulty interpretation of that clue and mess up the plan we'd already put into place. I supposed I'd just wait for Houston to show up this evening and see what he'd discovered during his trip to the King Leopold Charters headquarters.

By the time Houston arrived, I'd pretty much worked myself into a ball of nervous energy.

"What's wrong?" he asked.

I guessed that I hadn't done as good a job of hiding my nerves as I'd hoped.

"I had an incident today."

"Incident?"

I went on to explain about connecting with Shredder, the text I'd received, the detour to the marina, and the observations I'd made. I admitted that this little side trip had me wondering if the kidnapper had actually provided me with a clue to get me started or if I'd been getting close to something, and he'd sent me a distraction.

"I guess we now know that this guy has been tracking your cell phone as we suspected. Again, that isn't exactly a bad thing. I think we can use that to our advantage."

"I guess. The thing I'm not sure of at this point is whether or not we should stick to our plan to head to Seward tonight or if we should scrap that idea and head directly to Homer."

"It only takes about two and a half hours to drive to Seward from here. Even less since we'll be traveling at night when there shouldn't be any traffic. I'm going to suggest we stick to the plan. If that doesn't pan out, then we'll head to Homer tomorrow."

"Okay. That sounds like a good plan. Of course, I have no idea how we'll fit in sleep."

"We'll take turns driving. I'm going to suggest we take my car tonight since it will be best for yours to remain in the parking area, assuming this guy has eyes on the parking lot."

"Do you think he does?"

Houston shrugged. "The guy seems to be highly skilled, and you checked in under your own name, so I'm going to assume he's using hotel cameras to keep an eye on things. I'll drive to Seward while you catch a nap on the back seat. I'll leave my car in the parking area tomorrow, and you can drive to Homer, which is where the kidnapper should be expecting you to head next, and I'll sleep on the back seat. Once we get there, we can figure out the rest."

I took a minute to think things through, but I eventually agreed to Houston's plan.

"If this guy is watching parking lot security cameras, how am I going to get into your car?"

"I'll pull up to the door. We can use something to disguise you. Just keep your head down."

"There's a wheelchair in the lobby. Maybe you can just wheel me out. If I hide my face, the kidnapper shouldn't realize it's me in the wheelchair even if he is watching."

"Good idea. The wheelchair will provide a reason for me to pull up to the door as well."

Houston held up a bag that I just now realized he'd been holding. "I brought food. It seemed safer than ordering room service."

"Great. I'm starving. You can tell me about your day while we eat."

Houston set a large hamburger and a sleeve of fries in front of me before sitting down with an identical meal. "My day was mildly productive. I created a fake email and had the woman who helped me at King Leopold Charters email me quite a bit of information. I guess the company utilizes a variety of warehouses and storage units to handle all the company's equipment. I specifically asked about crabbing equipment and was told that there are storage units in Seward, Homer, and Ketchikan for all the seasonal equipment. Luckily, each of these storage buildings has an access code. I asked her to send me the list of access codes in the event I needed to check any of them out. I did tell the woman that I was pleased with my inspection of the corporate offices and wouldn't need to explore every outbuilding, just a select few. She seemed pleased with that."

I wiped a smear of ketchup from my mouth. "That's excellent. If you have the access codes, we won't have to break in anywhere."

"That's the idea."

"Anything else?" I asked as I sprinkled salt on my fries.

"I have maps of the locations of all the main and accessory buildings and storage units, as well as a key indicating which are used on a daily basis and which are accessed infrequently, which will help us to home in on those locations the kidnapper is most likely using to hide out in."

It sounded as if Houston had done what he'd set out to do. Now, all we had to do was hope that our plan paid off, and we found Shredder before it was too late.

Chapter 14

After we'd debriefed and enjoyed our burgers, Houston went down to the lobby and asked to borrow the wheelchair. He then brought his car to the front door. Once the car was in place, he met me in his room, which I'd accessed via the adjoining door. I had a blanket wrapped around me, so I didn't think I'd be identifiable even if I was caught on a camera. Once I was safely in the back seat, Houston returned the wheelchair, and then we headed toward Seward. There were only two buildings to check out in Seward, and only one of the two buildings was close to the dock. It was actually unlikely that the building on the water would be the one we were looking for, but Houston hadn't been wrong when he'd pointed out that the only way we could know for sure was to check.

As planned, I'd left my cell phone and computer in my room. If the kidnapper was watching, he would likely assume I'd stayed in for the evening.

The trip, it seemed, was going as planned. We'd made it to Seward in good time. Houston used his access codes to enter the two buildings owned by King Leopold Charters. As we expected, the building near the dock was a maintenance facility, which would have people going in and out every day. The other building, a storage unit, was much smaller and wouldn't be accessed on a daily basis, but after quickly peeking inside, I was able to determine that the building wasn't the one I'd seen in my dream or my connection with Shredder.

My head was pounding once again, so Houston recommended I lay down on the back seat and get some sleep. That seemed like a good idea, but what I hadn't expected was to connect with the man we were looking for while I slumbered.

"Ah. You did show up tonight. I hoped after we missed each other last night you wouldn't stay up all night fretting and miss tonight as well."

"You expected me last night?" I asked.

"I thought you might show up, but you didn't. How exactly does this work?"

"I have no idea," I answered honestly. "We only connect when I'm sleeping, and I never remember all of what was said."

"But you can see what I see."

Deciding to be honest with the man in an effort to gain his trust, I answered his query in my mind. "I guess I can, but it's dark tonight. I can hear your voice but can't see anything."

"I figured out that you could see what I see when you went looking at warehouses today, so I'm sitting in the dark."

That was unfortunate.

"I realize that I gave you a deadline, and you're motivated to meet that deadline, but I don't want to make it too easy."

"Since you brought this up," I said in my mind. "When exactly is this deadline?"

"Check your cell phone when you wake up."

"Speaking of phones, I assume you're the one who sent me to the marina today."

"Perhaps."

"Is the marina a clue, or was it a distraction? Was I getting close to something?"

"Time will tell. I need to go."

With that, he was gone.

"Are you okay back there?" Houston asked. "You were mumbling and thrashing about."

"I fell asleep, and during my sleep, I connected with the kidnapper."

Houston turned his head a bit. "What did he say?"

"Pull over. The guy thinks I'm all tucked into my bed. I think it's safe for me to ride in the front."

Houston did as I asked. Once we were back on the road, he asked me again about my conversation. I shared as much as I could remember, but as I'd told the kidnapper, I didn't always remember everything I dreamed.

"At this point, there are several possibilities," I said. "Either I was getting close to something, and the trip to the marina was nothing other than a distraction." I frowned. "I may have said something similar to this in my dream. It sounds familiar, but my memory is getting fuzzier by the minute. Another possibility is that there actually was a clue at the marina for me to find. I really don't know if the clue had to do with The Sea Witch or with Homer. The man who owns the boat was there when I arrived, so I stopped and spoke to him. This caused me to focus on his boat, but there were a lot of boats in the area. It's totally possible that the kidnapper sent me a clue, but I missed it since I was focused on the wrong thing." I let out a long slow breath. "This is really stressful. And confusing. I'm not sure what to do next."

"In the absence of a solid clue, I think we should follow the plan we already came up with. Our original plan was to head to Homer tomorrow. I think we should do that. I have a map that shows the locations of all the buildings owned by King Leopold Charters in Homer. I also have the access codes for those buildings. I say we check those out and then decide what to do."

"Okay, but I'll access the buildings. Alone," I emphasized. "If the clue sent to me by the kidnapper was for me to head to Homer, he'll be watching."

"I have a listening device you can wear. The kidnapper won't be able to see it, but it will allow me to communicate with you. You will be able to speak to me as well, but you'll want to be careful about talking if you're in a location where there might be a camera."

"Did you bring the device with you?"

"No. I got it from my friend with the ID and uniform."

I closed my eyes and rested my head on the seat behind me. I felt like there were things I really needed to remember but hadn't been able to. When I intentionally connected with someone, I was in charge of the connection and generally remembered everything I saw and everything that was said. But when I connected during my sleep, the experience was much more like a dream. Everything was very vivid at the time, but the images and details faded shortly after waking unless I wrote them down.

"So, what should we do at this point?" I asked as we pulled into the parking area for the hotel where we were staying. "Should we stay until morning, or should we head to Homer now?"

Houston turned the car off and then answered. "I think we should act as if you were simply following up on the clue to head to Homer. We should leave in the morning, taking your rental car and leaving mine behind. We should leave your cell phone on since the man seems to be tracking it, but I'm going to turn mine off so that he doesn't pick my signal up. We have our burner phones, and I have the surveillance equipment. It's about a four-hour drive to Homer. I'll lie down on the back seat while you drive. Once you arrive at the outskirts, we'll find a place that's assured to be camera-free to get organized."

"Okay." I agreed, glancing at the hotel Houston and I had checked into the previous evening.

"I guess we should go up separately."

"I think so," Houston agreed. "You go first. I'll wait a bit before going to my room."

"What time should we meet in the morning?"

"How about eight o'clock. I'll grab some breakfast and bring it up. Leave the door connecting our rooms open for me."

"Okay." I slipped out of the car and kept my head down as I accessed the building from a back door. Houston pulled around and parked the car. After waiting a few minutes, he entered the building via the front door. Upon entering my room, I'd initially forgotten all about checking my cell phone, but then I saw it sitting there on my bedside table. There was a new app on my phone. When I opened the app, a digital counter that was ticking down from four days, twenty hours, thirty-seven minutes, and twelve seconds appeared.

I glanced at the clock. Doing a quick calculation, I realized the man must have started the clock at midnight on the day I'd first spoken to him about Shredder.

I knocked on the adjoining door, hoping Houston was there. He opened the door with a startled look. "Is everything okay?"

I held up the cell phone.

"What am I looking at?" he asked.

"The amount of time, down to the second, that Shredder has left to live if we don't find him."

Chapter 15

Since the events of the previous day made me feel like the weight of the world was on my shoulders, I was pleased that the actual trip to Homer was uneventful. Houston laid down on the back seat as we agreed he would until we neared the city. I found a dirt road free of any possible traffic cams to turn off on. Once I verified that the car was well hidden, we both got out.

"Okay, so what do you want me to wear?" I asked.

Houston opened a box that contained an earpiece and a small microphone. "Tuck the earpiece into whichever ear feels more comfortable. You have long hair, so I'm going to suggest that we clip the microphone to your collar under your ear. Let your hair hang naturally over it."

I tucked the earpiece into my left ear. "Should we test it?"

Houston walked about fifty yards away and said something. I could hear him clearly. I answered him, and he verified that I was coming through clearly as well.

He handed me a list of addresses and access codes. He suggested that I allow him to feed me the access codes once we arrived at each facility. If someone saw me consulting a piece of paper to access each individual building, it might seem suspicious.

Once I was all hooked up, Houston returned to the back seat and laid down under a blanket again. I drove to the warehouse closest to the marina. Not only was it open today, but occupied as well. I went ahead and went inside, deciding to ask the men if they'd seen anyone fitting Shredder's description. I was pretty sure that Shredder wasn't currently being held here, and I doubted he'd ever been here. The facility was a busy place. The men I spoke to were polite but not helpful. Neither had seen Shredder nor were able to suggest another location I could search.

After I left the first facility, I headed to the second. It was a smaller storage unit several miles from the marina. It looked to be used to store equipment, but it didn't look at all like the storage area I'd seen in my dreams. At first, the fact that I recognized the third place I searched had seemed like a good thing. Once I told Houston that not only had I found the facility where Shredder was initially held before being moved to the dark room where I eventually connected with him, but that the facility was currently empty, he insisted on coming in and dusting for prints. The storage building had been accessed by a lot of different people, so I wasn't sure that dusting for prints would do any good, but I supposed Houston just wanted to feel as if he was contributing to our investigation today.

Of course, I realized what a really bad idea it had been to allow Houston to enter the building once I saw that an entire day had been erased from the countdown.

"Oh no," I said once I realized what had happened. "When I went into the storage building, there was still four days, eight hours, forty minutes, and twelve seconds left on the countdown. Now the counter says three days, seven hours, fifty-two minutes, and seventeen seconds. An entire day is gone."

Houston frowned.

"He must have had cameras in the building," I said.

I wasn't a hundred percent certain I was right until I received a text from a blocked number that simply said, "I told you no cops."

"I'm sorry," Houston said. "I guess I should have been more careful." He looked around. "I don't see any cameras."

"I don't either," I agreed. "But apparently, there are some hidden somewhere. What are we going to do?"

Houston slowly shook his head. "I guess let's head back to Anchorage. We'll figure it out from there."

By the time we arrived back at our hotel, less than three days and three hours remained on the clock.

"Assuming we don't do anything else that will cause our kidnapper to take time off the clock, we basically have until the day after tomorrow to find Shredder," I said. "That's not enough time. There are too many places left on our list to search. And we haven't even talked about the fact that we aren't even sure that Shredder is still being held in a King Leopold facility. What if this guy simply started off there but moved onto something else?"

Houston wrapped his arms around me and hugged me tightly. He just stood with his arms around me for at least two minutes. Eventually, he took a step back. "We're both exhausted," he said. "I'm going to suggest that we get something to eat and then take another look at things. Our original plan has us heading to Ketchikan tomorrow. Making the trip will take most of the day since we'll be limited to flight schedules. I guess we need to decide if that really is the best move at this point."

"I need to try to connect with Shredder again. I don't think this guy knows I've been able to make a connection, so hopefully, I can do so and still stay off the radar."

Houston picked up a room service menu. "Okay, but food first."

Houston logged onto his computer. I could see that he was looking at flights.

"There's a flight out of Anchorage to Ketchikan in two hours. There's a commuter to Juno at six-thirty tomorrow morning and a flight from Juno to Anchorage at ten a.m. That would allow us to search the buildings in both locations and still put us back here in plenty of time to put in a full day of searching if the Ketchikan thing doesn't work out."

"Are there tickets available? And what about a rental car? Can we get one in both Ketchikan and Juno?"

There was a knock on the door.

"I'll check while you get the food."

I did as Houston suggested. I really was exhausted, and simply going to bed and worrying about this whole thing tomorrow was tempting, but I wouldn't do that. There would be plenty of time to rest once Shredder was safe and the madman who took him was behind bars.

Once we'd settled in with our food, I made a suggestion that I knew wouldn't go over well. "I think I should go on this next leg of the journey alone."

"There's no way I'm going to allow you to walk into what is most likely a trap without backup."

I took a deep breath, held it, and blew it out slowly. "I understand your hesitation. I do. But we've already lost an entire day, and I don't think we can risk losing another. The flights you've found are limited, so we'd have to travel together. Me going first and you meeting me there isn't going to work this time. And since we have to show ID, it's not like we can use fake names. If you go, he'll know."

Houston didn't answer right away. At least he was thinking things over. I knew that he knew I was right, but I also knew that despite that, he wasn't going to let me walk into whatever I was walking into alone.

"Okay, what if I contact the police department in Juno and arrange for someone to meet you at the airport. I can do the same thing in Ketchikan."

"Sounds like a risk."

"Maybe, but it's the only option I can think of. Either I go with you, or you allow me to find someone who can."

There was no way I was going to get away with going alone, so eventually, I agreed to Houston's plan. It wasn't a perfect plan, and I was fully expecting fallout, but I really wasn't sure what my options were at this point. If I insisted on going alone, Houston would insist on coming along. I really wasn't sure how I could stop him.

"The cops need to be disguised as rideshare drivers. I will need transportation once I get to my destinations, so having drivers pick me up makes sense."

"Okay," Houston said. "You do what you need to do to get ready, and I'll make some calls."

I wasn't sure how he did it, but Houston arranged to have a taxi pick me up from the airport at each destination. The cab was from the local service, but the driver would actually be an armed cop. I had to admit I did feel a bit safer doing it this way than going alone.

Chapter 16

Houston's plan should have worked. It seemed as if he'd worked out all the details. And until I arrived back in Anchorage the following day, I actually thought it had. There hadn't been any additional time deducted from the countdown, and while I hadn't been able to connect with Shredder as I hoped, I had been really distracted, so, combined with the fact that he may very well have been unconscious when I tried, this outcome wasn't really surprising.

The negative to my otherwise uneventful overnight trip was that I hadn't found anything that helped us. By this point, I was pretty sure that the location where Shredder was currently being held was in no way connected to King Leopold Charters. Without this lead, which was the only one we had, I really wasn't sure how I was going to save Shredder in the next two days.

"Houston, are you here?" I called out after entering my room and knocking on the adjoining door. When no one answered, I tried the door, which was unlocked. The room was empty, but all of Houston's stuff was still there. I supposed he might have gone out for breakfast, or he'd taken a walk. At this point, all I really wanted was a shower and a quick power nap, so I left a note for Houston to let him know that I was back and that I was going to close my eyes for an hour. I asked that he wake me by noon if I wasn't already awake.

Setting my cell phone on the bedside table, I watched the timer count down for a full minute. I had no idea how I was going to find Shredder, but there was no way I was going to let him die. I hated to take even an hour to rest, but I hadn't had any decent sleep for days and felt weak and shaky. Hopefully, a hot shower and an hour of shuteye would be enough to get me through the next thirty-six hours.

To be honest, as I dozed off, I really hadn't expected to connect with the kidnapper. I was only going to take a quick nap and wasn't sure that I'd even be able to reach the level of REM sleep required to connect, so I was surprised to not only hear his voice but see the room he was in through his eyes as well.

"Seems like you had a long night," he said.

So he had been watching. "I did." I tried to focus on what I could see as I answered him in my mind. "I can't say that I got anywhere, but you have to give me points for trying."

"I'm afraid any points you may have earned with your dogged determination have been erased due to your consistent tendency to cheat."

My heart rate increased. I wanted to wake myself up to check the countdown on my cell phone, but I felt hopeless to do so. "I didn't cheat," I said, knowing it wasn't true. "Houston stayed here, and I went alone."

"It was a clever ruse, but we both know that the taxi drivers who carted you around weren't actually taxi drivers at all. I'm really not sure why you're making this harder than it needs to be."

Good question. "What can I do to make things right."

The kidnapper got up and walked across a huge room that appeared to be littered with boxes stacked one atop the other. When he arrived at the far end of the room, he opened a door, revealing a smaller room with both Shredder and Houston splayed out on the floor.

I couldn't help but gasp. "Are they alive?"

"They are. For now, at least. Once you hooked up with the police in Juno, I realized that your cop friend would continue to cause problems as long as he was allowed to stay in the game. The rules are the same as they've always been, although now you have two lives to save. Find your friends before the timer runs down, or they both die."

I wanted to be brave, but even in my dream state, I wasn't able to prevent the tears that streamed down my face.

"Now, now, none of that," he said. "You still have time. How about a clue to get you started?"

"Yes. Please. A clue would be appreciated."

"Clue number one is that I'm still in Alaska. Since you've been away for hours, you must realize that conceivably I've had time to move the men a great distance, so I'm going to narrow this down for you. I'm going to send you a GPS location. Go to the location indicated and look for a clue."

"A clue? What sort of clue?"

The man actually chuckled. "I can't do everything for you, now can I?"

With that, he was gone, and I was awake. I realized when I woke that not only had I been able to connect with the kidnapper a lot more clearly than I had in the beginning, but I was beginning to not only see what he saw but feel what he felt as well. I was also able to hear echoes from his mind. I wasn't sure if I was picking up his current thoughts or memories, but I realized that tapping into whatever he had going on was going to give me the motive for what he'd spent the past few months doing, which hopefully would help me find the men I was looking for.

Before getting up, I took a minute to get my bearings and try to figure out what to do. My head felt fuzzy, and my mind blurry. I quickly wrote down everything I remembered from my dream. I remembered the large room with the stacks of boxes. It looked like the interior of an abandoned shop of some sort. I didn't think we were dealing with another warehouse. This building felt smaller. If I had to guess, the larger room where the man was standing had been a storefront or maybe a restaurant, which had since closed, and the smaller room where Shredder and Houston had been passed out had perhaps been an office or storage room of some sort.

I tried to remember what the man had been thinking. What he'd been feeling. I could sense both pain and excitement. I'd picked up deep anguish, which had somehow been mixed up with a feeling of longing and regret. There was an echo of a name. Sarah. I wasn't sure who Sarah was, but for the first time, I had a knowing that it was grief for this woman that drove the man to do what he had. I needed to try to explore that. My intuition told me that knowing the why of this whole thing was going to help me put an end to it.

I got up and crossed the room. The man had said he'd send me a GPS location. I looked at my cell phone and found a text waiting to be opened. The GPS location provided was just south of Wasilla. Grabbing both cell phones, along with my computer and suitcase, I headed out to my rental car. Wasilla was about an hour away. I just hoped that I recognized the clue once I arrived and knew what to do with it.

Chapter 17

Traffic was heavy, so the trip took a few minutes longer than I'd planned, but eventually, I arrived at a bar and grill. What I hadn't been expecting was for the bar and grill to be open and busy with the lunch crowd.

"Okay, now what?" I mumbled to myself. Why would the kidnapper send me to a location full of people? Deciding to head to the front reception counter, I asked the hostess if someone might have left something behind for pickup.

"Oh, you must be Harmony." The friendly young woman smiled.

"I am Harmony. Harmony Carson. Do you have something for me?"

She handed me an envelope.

"Who dropped this off?" I asked.

She furrowed her brow. "I'm not sure exactly. I didn't work the late shift yesterday, but Max, the closing bartender, told me that some guy came in just before last call and gave him five hundred dollars to pass this envelope along to a woman with dark hair that would come looking for it the following day."

"Did Max say what this man looked like?"

"Tall. Dark hair. Sort of a raspy voice."

Sounded like our guy. "Was anyone with him?"

"No. I don't think so. At least Max didn't mention anyone else."

"What time would he have been here?"

She shrugged. "I don't know exactly. We closed at eleven last night, so I'm going to say somewhere between ten and eleven since Max said he was getting ready to start closing up." She glanced at the envelope in my hand. "So what's in there anyway?"

I glanced down at what I hoped would be the next clue. "I'm not sure. I don't suppose I might be able to speak to Max."

"He's probably at home. I can give you his cell phone number. I'm not promising he'll pick up. He doesn't always, but he might."

I took the number and envelope and headed back to my car. I sat in the parking lot as I opened the envelope. There was a photo of a gas station that looked to have been abandoned for years. The pumps were old, and I was sure inoperable. The building beyond the pumps was boarded up. There was a sign above the door of the building that announced that there were no public bathrooms. If I had to guess, the facility hadn't been in operation for more than a decade. Probably more like two or three decades based on the antique-looking pumps. Offhand, I wasn't sure where the building might be located, but while the kidnapper had said no cops, he hadn't actually said no help, so I supposed I could take a photo of the photo I was holding in my hand with my cell phone and send it to Jake and the gang. Maybe someone would know what I was looking at.

I then called Max, who told me that the man who'd stopped by the previous evening had been driving a white panel van. Okay, that provided a clue of sorts. Max didn't notice the license plate, and he didn't remember there being writing of any sort on the vehicle, but he did say that the van was old. Really old. Like something from the sixties.

I took a moment to gather my thoughts. Okay, it seemed that the kidnapper came to the hotel where Houston and I were staying and kidnapped Houston at some point after I left. He was driving an old panel van and seemed to be heading north. He'd stopped at the bar and grill in Wasilla and left the envelope with the photo for me. Based on what Max had told me, this had most likely been around ten-thirty the previous evening. When I'd last connected with the kidnapper, he'd been in a building, not in a van or vehicle of any sort, so I had to assume he'd arrived at his destination. He'd stopped and left the photo more than fourteen hours ago, so based on an average speed of sixty miles an hour, he really could be almost anywhere. Well, not anywhere. He said he was still in Alaska, so if he was telling the truth, that eliminated the possibility of his heading into Canada. And unless he had access to a plane or helicopter, he had a limited number of roads to travel on in this part of the state. Still, the network of road options was much too vast to be explored before the timer ran out in less than a day and a half. Shredder and Houston would be dead in less than a day and a half if I didn't figure this out.

Making a decision, I texted the photo to Jake and then called him to explain that I needed him to try to help me find the physical location of the deserted gas station in the photo the kidnapper had left for me. I decided not to mention that Houston was no longer with me. That would only freak him out, and there really wasn't much he could do to help me, other than helping me with the clues, of course. Jake assured me he'd take the photo I'd texted him and show it around. If nothing else, maybe Landon could do something with it.

While I waited for Jake to get back to me, I paused to consider what to do. Staying put until I heard back made it feel like I was wasting time, but the reality was that there were several choices available to me in terms of a direction to head. I could head east toward Copper City. From there, I could veer south toward Valdez or north toward Tok.

I also had the option of continuing toward Talkeetna. It was close, and if the kidnapper wanted to reduce the amount of time he spent on the road with his hostages, it would make a good stop for him.

I could also continue on Hwy 3 toward Fairbanks. The road would be crazy with tourists at this time of the year, so in my opinion, not the best choice, but there were places along the way to stop or turn off.

And finally, while the kidnapper had sent me north from Anchorage, he could have doubled back and headed toward the Kenai Peninsula. There really were too many choices to just head out in a random direction without a plan.

Pulling out the original photo that had been left for me, I took a closer look at it. Maybe there was something in the background I'd recognize. If I knew the general direction to head, I could at least get back on the road. Of course, the scenery beyond the deserted building was limited by the way the photo was cropped, but I did notice mountains. There were a lot of mountains in Alaska, but mountains in the background were still a clue.

Thirty minutes after I'd sent the photo to Jake, he called me back.

"Landon said the building in the photo is up near Cantwell. He said to take Hwy 3 north and then turn east on Hwy 8."

I did a quick calculation. Cantwell was about three hours north if the traffic was light. It would be congested with people visiting Denali National Park, so it could take more like four hours. I supposed I should get going.

"Okay, thanks, Jake."

"Do you feel like you're getting close?"

I let out a long breath. "I'm not sure. Sometimes it feels like it, and other times I realize I have no idea what I'm doing."

"What does Houston think?"

"He thinks we'll find our guy. Look, I need to go. Thanks again. I'll call back if I need anything."

I hung up and then decided to go back inside to order food and a drink to go. I also decided to use the ladies' room since the further north you traveled, the greater the distance was between stops. Not only was I exhausted, but I really had no idea where this journey would take me. I wished I had even a little confidence to urge me on, but by this point, I felt myself die a tiny bit with each second that ticked down.

If there were traffic cams or security cameras, he could hack into them to watch me.

Chapter 18

The drive north was gorgeous, not that I noticed, given my heightened state of anxiety. If I hadn't been fighting for the lives of my friends, I might have taken the time to enjoy one of the many hiking trails or view one of the dozens of waterfalls. The scenery was some of the most breathtaking anywhere, but all I could see were images of the seemingly lifeless bodies of my friends viewed through the eyes of the kidnapper from my last dream.

As it was every summer, the road between Anchorage and Fairbanks was crazy with tourists. It was early in the season, so the peak crowds had yet to arrive. Still, it took me quite a bit longer to reach the sparsely traveled gravel road I was to turn off on than I'd anticipated. By the time I arrived at the deserted gas station, which thankfully was where Jake indicated it would be, it was already dinner time. Parking my car off to the side, I stepped out onto the pavement that was covered with potholes and tried to decide what to do next.

The building hadn't been occupied for a very long time. The roof sagged, and I wasn't even sure if it was safe to go inside. Deciding to walk around the exterior before trying to find a way in, I grabbed a jacket to block the chill that seemed to have come from nowhere and walked toward the front of the building. The large windows in the front had been boarded up. The exterior walls were covered with dirty beige stucco, and the dirt areas, which I assumed at one point, might have been used to display shrubs and seasonal flowers, were now overgrown with weeds. Standing at the front of the building, I turned and looked back toward the road. Two pumps I was sure had rusted through years ago were featured side by side on an island that served to divide the two fueling lanes. I could almost imagine the small facility in its heyday. The road had never been the main artery, but it had been used as a means of access to the National Park before it had become the popular travel location that it was today.

Once I felt I had a general feel for the area, I walked around the building in a clockwise direction. I took my time so as not to miss a possible clue. There was graffiti on one wall, but the paint looked weathered, so I doubted the kidnapper would use the messages scrawled on the wall as the vital piece of information I was after.

After I'd traveled the entire exterior of the building, I looked for a way in. The door was locked, and the windows boarded, so it was apparent that I'd need to break in. I hated to leave a path of destruction behind me, so I started by trying to pick the lock. When that didn't work, I looked around for something to use to pry one of the boards covering the windows loose. Perhaps I should have taken the time to stop for tools. At least a basic set that would provide me the assistance I needed to get into the vacant buildings I felt sure I was to encounter along the way. There wasn't a store that might carry what I needed for miles, so I decided to do the best I could with the sturdy stick and heavy rock I'd decided on.

Prying the huge piece of plywood loose from the window it had been covering for years wasn't easy, but I persisted, and eventually, the covering was removed. I felt bad about breaking the glass in order to get in but thought I had little choice. Once inside, I took a minute to get my bearings.

A counter with a metal surface was located toward the front of the building. There were shelves built in rows beyond that. The shelves were empty, but I imagined they'd been used to display oil and other supplies at one point. There was an old soda dispenser and a rack that had probably been used to hold chips or candy bars.

The dark brown tile was chipped and cracked, the walls covered in dust and grime, and the backdoor padlocked. Funny, I didn't remember seeing a back door when I'd taken my walk around the building. Perhaps there had been something stacked in front of it. I had noticed an excess amount of wooden pallets and worn tires randomly stacked behind the facility.

"Okay, so where is the clue?" I said aloud. I wasn't even sure if I'd find it inside the building or somewhere outside, but the dust on the floor looked to have been undisturbed before I'd entered the building, so based on this evidence, I had to assume the kidnapper hadn't been inside. That meant I needed to take another look around outside.

After climbing out through the broken window, I stood completely still and tried to imagine what the kidnapper might have been thinking. He had me taking a really tense road trip for some reason. I wasn't sure if this had always been his plan or if he had adapted his original plan after taking Houston as a hostage. I supposed the purpose of this game was to punish me, or perhaps it was simply to get to know me. If he wanted to kill Shredder, he could easily have done so. My suspicion was that Shredder hadn't even been on his original list and was simply a victim of opportunity.

"Okay, so what is it I'm supposed to be looking for?"

Of course, there was no one to answer, so I decided to walk around the exterior again. I'd really hoped this clue would be as easy to find as the clue at the bar and grill had been. I was exhausted, and my energy was fading fast. What I needed was sleep. My logical mind told me that a couple hours of sleep might go a long way toward clearing my mind enough for me to figure this out. The emotional part of my mind felt panic at the thought of wasting a single moment when so much was at stake.

I walked around the building three more times before finally deciding to try connecting with Shredder and Houston. If either man was conscious and I was able to get through, maybe they'd be able to provide a clue to help me make sense of things. I hadn't seen a single car go by since I'd been here, so I simply climbed into my car, locked the doors, set the timer on my cell phone for one hour in the event I fell asleep, and then closed my eyes and focused.

"Shredder," I said in my mind, deciding to start with the man I'd had previous success connecting with. "Are you there?" I pictured his image, hoping that he wasn't too drugged up to receive me. "It's Harmony. Can you hear me?"

I gave it fifteen minutes before I decided to switch my focus to Houston. After nearly thirty minutes of unsuccessfully trying to connect with him, my head was pounding. I reset my timer for another hour and then allowed myself to drift off to sleep.

"Sleeping?" he asked in an almost condescending tone of voice.

"I just needed a few minutes. This would go a lot better if you'd get out of my head."

"I actually think you're in my head."

I supposed the man had a point.

"I'm not sure what the point of this whole thing is, and I really can't decide if you want me to succeed or fail, but I do know that if I can't get a few minutes of quality sleep, I'm going to lose my mind," I said.

"Understood. I guess I'll let you get back to it."

"Wait. I'm at the abandoned gas station. What am I supposed to find?"

"The message beneath."

With that, he was gone, and unfortunately, I was awake.

I groaned and then opened my eyes. I needed to write down my impressions before they faded the way dreams tended to do. I remembered him telling me to look for the message beneath. I also remembered seeing the walls behind him. Wood. No, not just wood; logs. A log cabin. Okay, that was helpful. The problem was that there were a lot of log cabins in this part of the state. Too many to track down and check out. I'd need to figure out the other clue.

I sat up and looked around. We didn't get much darkness at this time of the year, but the few hours we did get would hamper my ability to find whatever it was I needed to find. It made sense for me to get up and look around now. I could find a place to sleep during the dark hours. Getting out of the car, I stood in front of the building, staring at the sagging roof again as I tried to decide what I needed to do.

The message beneath.

Beneath what? Beneath the piles of tires and wooden pallets? Beneath the rows of empty shelves? Beneath the counter that I assumed had once held a cash register? I pulled my cell phone out and looked at the minutes counting down. One day, one hour, twenty-seven minutes, and thirteen seconds. My stomach clenched, and I resisted the urge to throw up. I needed more time. A lot more time. Fighting the urge to have a total meltdown, I decided to walk around the exterior of the building once again. I'd already decided that it hadn't appeared that anyone had been inside, so if there was a clue to find, it was likely I'd find it out here.

It took over an hour before I realized there was something beneath the graffiti on the wall. Whatever had been committed to the wall so long ago had endured years of some of the most severe weather anywhere in the country, so what existed had likely been chipped and faded even before the graffiti covered it. What I needed, I decided, was a photo of the building before the graffiti was applied. I took my cell phone out. The cell service was almost nonexistent, but I finally got a weak cell signal after walking around with my phone over my head for about twenty minutes. Not enough to use the internet and probably not enough to make a call, but maybe enough to send a text. I quickly sent a text to both Landon and Jake, asking them to forward me a photo of the deserted gas station before it was deserted if they had one. It was late, almost midnight, but given the fact that he owned and operated a bar, Jake was the sort to stay up late.

It took nearly twenty minutes, but eventually, a text came through from Landon. The text included a photo of the gas station before it had been closed down. On the wall was a map that showed Hwy 8 between Hwy 3 and Hwy 4 that was illustrated to show features along the road, including buildings. There was a star where the gas station was located, and there were tiny cabins painted on the wall, which I imagined represented the cabins that existed at the time the map was painted.

"Okay," I said aloud. "It looks like all I need to do is figure out which of these seasonal hunting cabins the kidnapper is hiding out in."

I glanced back toward the car. It was going to be dark soon. I set the timer on my watch for four hours, sent a return text to Landon thanking him and assuring him that things were going well, and then I climbed into my car, locked the doors, and faded off to sleep.

Chapter 19

I'd really needed uninterrupted sleep and felt much better when I awoke until I realized the counter had wound down to less than twenty hours.

I pulled up the photo Landon had sent me and studied it. There weren't a lot of cabins, and if I'd had more time, I would have simply searched each one from the closest to my current location to the furthest. But I didn't have much time. I supposed that many of the cabins still stood, but others would have been damaged by fires and blizzards. I wasn't sure how many were currently occupied, but that would be good information to possess. Neither Jake nor Landon would be up yet, and I still didn't have strong enough service to make a call, but I figured I could text them now and ask them to text me later. I warned them that

I was out of range and may not respond right away, so not to worry if it took me a while. I promised I'd get back to them when I was able.

"Okay, Harm, what now?" I asked myself aloud.

I knew that Max had seen the kidnapper in a white panel van. If the kidnapper's objective was not to be found, the van would be well hidden, but if the objective of the man was to lure me into a trap, then the van would be sitting in front of the cabin for all to see. The total distance between the two towns that bookended the highway was a hundred and thirty-five miles. Most of the cabins were located along the main road, although there were a few tucked away at the end of rutted dirt roads. The road was rough, mostly gravel, so the speed I'd be able to travel would be limited, but I still figured I could make it to the town on the other end in less than five hours. Five hours would still leave me almost fourteen to save the guys, so it might be worth the time it took to get a feel for things. I also hoped I'd hear from either Jake or Landon by then. I wasn't sure that heading off on a five-hour road trip was the most efficient use of my time, but I was totally out of ideas, so I decided to take a chance and go for it.

And my plan hadn't been a bad one. I hadn't had time to look inside any of the cabins, but I had determined which cabins along the main road appeared to be occupied. I used the photo of the map on the wall as a guide, and by the time I got to Paxson, I had the list of possible cabins where the kidnapper might be hiding out narrowed down a bit.

Deciding to fill my tank and my stomach, I pulled up to the only gas station in town. It was then that texts from Landon, as well as Jake, came through. I set up a group text and texted them back. I told them I'd try to call. Landon said he'd head to Neverland, where Jake was doing paperwork so they could both talk to me. I told them that I was going to grab some food, and providing the cell service was strong enough, I would call them in thirty minutes. If not, I'd text.

"Ham and cheese sandwich and a cola, please," I said to the woman behind the counter of the tiny store. She handed me my purchases, and I headed out to my car to eat. By the time I finished eating, the thirty minutes were up, so I called Neverland. Thankfully, Jake answered.

"So, what's going on?" Jake asked. I could hear the worry in his voice. I was tempted to tell him what was really going on, but I knew that if he knew what had actually happened, he'd have Dani bring him down in the chopper. I was terrified that doing so would break the crazy contract I seemed to have entered into with the kidnapper. He'd already deducted a full day from the total and taken Houston hostage in response to what he considered to be unwarranted help and interference, so I decided not to risk it.

"We're making progress," I answered my brother-in-law. "Houston is grabbing some sleep while I try to narrow down the possible choices for the location of the next clue."

"So you think the next clue will be in one of these cabins?" Landon asked.

"Based on the information I have available to me at this point, that's exactly what I think. I took a drive from the old abandoned gas station to Paxson. I managed to narrow things down a bit, but I hoped you could narrow things down a bit more. Do you have that program that provides an aerial view in real-time?"

"I do. You want to know which cabins still exist and of those that still exist which look as if they might be occupied and which are vacant."

"Basically," I answered.

"So I imagine you expect to find the clue in an unoccupied cabin," Jake said.

"That's my guess," I answered, although, by this point, it really came down to motivation. If the kidnapper didn't want me to find them, there wouldn't be woodsmoke or other sign of occupancy. If he did want me to find them, he'd have a cheery fire sending smoke through the valley.

"Maybe it's time to call someone in," Jake said. "The Feds, maybe."

"Houston and I have discussed that and have decided that if we can't find Shredder by the end of the day tomorrow, we'll do just that." I figured that one way or another, this would all be over by the end of the day today. "I appreciate you guys helping out, but we have this. Just get me the aerial information

I'm looking for and text it to me. The service is really spotty. I'm not sure I'll be able to call again."

Jake spent a couple more minutes trying to convince me that I should try to get help, but eventually, I pretended I lost him and hung up.

It didn't take Landon long to send the information I'd asked for. I studied the list he sent and compared it to the list I'd already made of existing versus no longer existing cabins, as well as probably occupied versus probably vacant cabins. After taking everything into consideration, I finally decided on a small grouping of cabins nestled near a lake about five miles off the main road. I figured it would take me about an hour to drive to the road leading to the cabins. At that point, I'd travel part of the way along the dirt road and then hide my car and walk the rest of the way in. If the kidnapper was there, I'd take a minute to figure out my next move. If he wasn't there, I'd need to move quickly onto Plan B. Boy, I wished I had the day left that I'd lost as a punishment for allowing Houston to help me.

Chapter 20

The drive along the gravel road toward the dirt road that would take me out to the lake was a pretty one. A herd of caribou crossed the road in front of me just a mile after I'd noticed a mama moose and her baby standing off to the side of the road grazing. I loved the long days of summer. There was something about them that felt magical. Almost surreal.

I thought about my pack of dogs, wondering how they were doing with Serena. The dogs loved my cheerful friend, but I knew that they'd be missing me by now. Denali always seemed to know when I was in any sort of danger. Chances were he was pacing about, waiting for me to come home. And while Moose could be downright crotchety at times, he also had a knack for knowing my moods. While he wasn't the sort to want to cuddle during ordinary moments if

I needed him, he was right there to lend his energy and support.

God, I missed them all.

I brushed a tear from my cheek. While I longed with all my heart to be home in my own corner of the world, I knew at this moment I was where I needed to be. The fact that I was in this situation was crazy. In fact, my life seemed to be getting crazier and crazier as my "gift" grew and evolved. There were times I longed for the simpler days before I'd been able to connect with killers in my dreams. I longed for the comfort of ignorance from the pain and cruelty these individuals had brought to my life.

I slowed to around ten miles an hour as I neared the location where the map on my cell phone indicated the dirt road would be. Since cell service kept fading in and out, updates to my map kept fading in and out, so I knew I couldn't count on timely directions.

Once I turned onto the narrow rutted road, I drove slowly for about four miles, pulled my car behind a grove of dense brush, and got out. I needed the element of surprise if I was going to make any plan work, so I took my time and moved silently through the shrubs and trees.

I paused as the five cabins came into view. They were spaced within the line of sight of each other, so I'd need to be extra careful as I approached in an attempt to determine occupancy.

"Okay, Harm, now what?" I whispered to myself. I really couldn't see how I was going to obtain access to any of the cabins while remaining hidden from the other four. I still had time and didn't want to act rashly, so I decided to pause where I was for a moment. I was well hidden yet could see the partial exterior of all five cabins. Maybe I'd just watch for a bit and see if I just happened to notice movement of any sort.

Finding a comfortable place to sit, I leaned against a tree and closed my eyes. "Are you there?" I said to myself as I focused on Shredder. "I know you are in a tough spot, but I really need you. Please hear me."

I let tears roll down my cheeks as I thought about my mysterious friend. I hated that he might die before I'd even had the chance to learn his real name. Not that knowing his real name was all that important. And while the man was often nothing more than a shadow drifting in and out in my life and never really staying long, I had to admit that he was one of the most important people to occupy space in my small and isolated world.

"I know if you were here, you'd know exactly what to do, but I have no idea, and I'm scared. Really scared. Please, Shredder. I need you. Wake up and help me!"

I waited and listened. I focused even harder. If I could wake Shredder by sheer will, I would.

"Harm?" he finally came through just as my head felt it was about to explode with the pain.

"I'm here. I need help. Please try to stay conscious."

"Okay. I'll do what I can. Catch me up."

"There is less than ten hours left on the countdown. The kidnapper has both you and Houston, so I'm alone. I'm scared, and I have no idea what to do."

"Take a breath," he said in my head. "I'm going to help you. We have this, but you need to relax."

"Okay," I said, even though relaxing was out of the question at this point.

"Where are you?"

I told him about the five cabins and my hope that the kidnapper was holding them in one of them. I admitted that I hadn't been able to verify that at this point, but based on the information I had, one of these cabins as the holding place seemed to be the best option.

"Okay, the first thing we need to do is verify if we are in one of the cabins and, if so, which one. I'm going to walk you through it, but first, let's go over a few other things."

"Okay. What do I need to know?"

"To this point, the kidnapper has been keeping me drugged up most of the time, but he's also been allowing me to wake to give me food and water. Once I've eaten, he gives me another shot of the sedative. I've mostly gone along with this, but the next time he comes in with the food, I'm going to pretend not to wake up. I'm hoping he'll assume he's given me too much and skip the injection."

"Okay. That sounds like a good plan."

"I know that at times you connect with him. He may try to test me in order to determine whether or not I'm faking. He may cut or kick me or do something to cause me to flinch if, in fact, I'm not fully under. I can withstand that, but I need you to withstand it as well. Don't try to save me. Just let things play out."

"Wait. Don't try to save you? What do you mean?"

"I guess I mean, don't try to save me yet. In order for my plan to work, we need to wait until the very last minute to act. During the very last minutes of the countdown, the kidnapper, Houston, and I should all be physically located in the same space. Chances are that as the timer counts down the last minutes, the killer will wake Houston and me so we can be part of the show. He'll want us to know that you failed. He'll want us to know that we only have seconds to live. It's while he's distracted by this that we'll make our move."

"Move?" I started to hyperventilate. "What move?"

"You distract him, and I'll disarm him."

"Distract him?" I squeaked. "How?"

"Use your imagination. Listen, I need to go. I can hear movement on the other side of the door. If my plan works, I should be able to resist being drugged again. Try to connect with me in an hour. I'm hoping we'll have a better feel for things by then. In the meantime, stay low and out of sight, but look for the van. If the guy is here, he has to have it stashed somewhere."

With that, he was gone.

Chapter 21

Alone again, I took several deep breaths. I wanted to curl into a ball and sob, but I knew that wouldn't get me anywhere. Shredder had told me to figure out a way to prove that the kidnapper was holed up in one of the cabins, so that was what I was going to do. Taking a minute to get the lay of the land, I plotted out a route in my mind then headed through the trees and underbrush to look for the van. It took me over an hour, but eventually, I was able to find the vehicle parked behind a storage shed of some sort located behind the second to the last cabin in the grouping.

Blowing out a deep breath, I made my way back to my original hiding spot. Finding the van was huge. At least I knew I was on the right track. But I still didn't know which, if any, of the five cabins were occupied. So far, I hadn't seen evidence of another living soul. No woodsmoke. No movement or noise. Nothing to help narrow things down.

Once I was settled back in my hiding spot, I tried to connect with Shredder again.

"Are you there?" I queried despite my massive headache.

"I'm here. My plan worked. The man didn't give me an injection when he was in since I hadn't yet regained consciousness. Or at least as far as he knows, I wasn't conscious."

"And Houston?"

"He was fed and then injected. I suspect he will remain drugged up until the time arrives for the final showdown. The kidnapper seems to have something to wake us up when he wants to."

I said a silent prayer of thanks that both men were still okay.

"Did you find the van?" he asked.

"I did. It's behind a shed, which is located behind the second cabin from the right. I don't know if that means that he chose the second cabin from the right to wait for me or if he simply thought the shed would be a good structure to park behind."

"We will need to figure out which of the five cabins we're locked up in, but before we get to that, are you okay? I know how these psychic connections give you a headache."

"I'm fine. Don't worry about me. Are you okay?"

"I'm fine. The guy kicked me around a bit in an attempt to verify that I really was unconscious, but I was expecting worse. I'm hoping I won't see him again until he comes back to wake us at the end of the countdown."

"Are you sure he'll wake you and make a production out of it? He could just come in and shoot you in the head without bothering to wake you."

"No, I'm not sure, but I think he'll wake us. The guy seems to be in this for the thrill it brings to his life. I don't think that taking Houston or me was part of his original plan. I don't think either of us is on his list. If I had to guess, the idea that you were able to connect with him in your dream state intrigued him, and he decided to play with that a bit. If you don't make it in time to save us, he'll be disappointed. And fair warning, he'll likely come after you directly, so in the event my plan fails, you need to get gone. Change your name and move far, far away."

Of course, this had me panicking once again, but I decided not to think about it. "I won't fail. Our plan won't fail. What do you want me to do next?"

"Give me a few minutes. I'm going to break the connection, but I want you to try again in one hour. If I don't answer in an hour, wait another hour and try again. Keep trying until I answer, but wait an hour between each effort. I don't want to tire you out, and there may be a good reason why I can't answer."

"Okay. And in the meantime?"

"In the meantime, stay out of sight, but continue watching the cabins for any sign of light or movement."

"Okay. Be careful."

With that, I was once again alone. I pulled my cell phone out and looked at the clock counting down. Eight hours, four minutes, and twelve seconds.

Chapter 22

At the moment that my fifth attempt to connect with Shredder failed, I wanted to give up. I wanted to storm up to the door of the cabin closest to me and plead with the man I hoped was inside to show mercy. But I knew my effort would be fruitless and would likely end in all our deaths, so I waited. Shredder had said to keep trying, but only once per hour, so despite the urgency I felt, I simply sat and prayed and waited.

When the sixth hour came and went, and I still hadn't connected, I considered a short nap. I could set my timer for fifty minutes and close my eyes. I wasn't sure if an attempt to connect with the kidnapper was a good idea, but by this point, I really needed to get a peek at what was going on for my own sanity, so I decided to take a risk.

"I was wondering if you'd show up," the kidnapper said in my dream. "Are you here to plead for mercy?"

"Would it help?"

"No. I'm afraid the rules of the game have been set. Are you still trying to find us?"

"I am, but you've done a good job of hiding. I don't suppose you want to send another clue in my direction?"

"No. At this point, success or failure is up to you. I will be sorry if you fail. I've come to enjoy these little chats."

The man I was channeling got up and began to pace around the room. That was good. It gave me a chance to pick up any clues in the environment. It also seemed to indicate that he was nervous for some reason.

"I need to see Shredder and Houston," I said. "I've realized that even if I find you, I may very well be walking into a trap. If the men are dead already, then I'll have no motivation to continue."

"They're alive."

"I need to see them. Through your eyes."

"And if I don't show you?"

"Then I guess I call in the Feds and head home."

The guy did another rotation around the room before answering. Eventually, he headed down a short hallway with only two doors. I supposed one led to a bathroom and one to a bedroom. The room the man had been in had featured a living area and a small kitchenette. The appliances were old and didn't appear to be functional, and the only furniture in the main section of the room was a torn sofa. The man opened the door to the right. There was a board over the window, making it dark but still light enough to see what I'd come to see. I almost lost the connection when I saw both men lying on the floor.

"Are they alive?"

"They are. Both men are unconscious for now, but I assure you they are alive."

Houston looked fine, but Shredder looked like he'd just finished a boxing match. "What happened to Shredder?"

The man hesitated.

"Tell me if you want me to continue."

"He didn't wake this morning as he should have. I may have overdone it with the sedative. I checked, and he's breathing fine, and his heart rate is good. He'll wake eventually."

"Why all the blood and bruising?"

"I had to make sure he wasn't faking."

Shredder had been correct. The guy had tested him.

"Did you give him more sedative? If he already had too much, another dose could kill him."

"I didn't give him more. He's out cold. I'm just hoping I can wake him for the finale, which," he said while looking at his watch, "is less than two hours away." He closed the door and walked back into the main room. "I'm going to sign off now, but you should wake up. I'm surprised you're sleeping when you have so little time left."

I woke as soon as the connection was broken.

The fact that I hadn't been able to connect with Shredder again left me feeling terrified, but in general, I knew he was alive, and I knew what I was supposed to do. I was supposed to wait until only minutes were left on the timer, and then I was to provide a distraction. I expected the man to be ready for almost anything I might try, so I knew that simply driving my car into the cabin or finding a way to make a loud noise wouldn't do it. I needed something more. I needed to find a way to shove him off his axis if only for the second it would take for Shredder to do what he needed to do.

I considered approaching the cabin at the last minute, but that seemed risky, and at this point, I still wasn't sure which cabin they were holed up in. While I wanted to save my friends, I didn't want to get myself killed in the process. I walked back to my car and climbed inside. I had a little over an hour left, and I needed to figure this out. I took out the notepad where I'd been jotting down the details in my dreams to help me remember.

Sarah. My notes had said that the kidnapper felt great grief over the loss of this woman and that it was this loss that had driven the man to do what he had. I'd also noted that my intuition suggested that my knowing this was the key to putting an end to everything that was going on.

How could I have forgotten this? I reread my notes, and suddenly I knew exactly what to do.

Chapter 23

Trying to figure out the perfect time to begin and then getting everything put into place from my seat in the car had caused me more angst than I'd ever experienced in the past. When the time I decided on finally arrived, I made myself comfortable then tried to intentionally connect with the man for the first time. It took a few tries, and I knew I was running out of time, but this was the only play in my playbook, so I gave it everything I had.

What I needed to do was to get in but not let the man know I was in. Not an easy task but one I had accomplished in the past with other individuals.

By the time I was finally connected with the kidnapper, both Shredder and Houston were standing in the cabin's main room. The kidnapper stood in front of them, and while I couldn't see a gun, I could sense one. I also sensed that the kidnapper hadn't yet noticed me lurking around in his mind.

"One minute and twelve seconds," the kidnapper said to the hostages.

Houston looked both groggy and terrified, but I swear Shredder was actually suppressing a grin.

"Something funny?" the man asked.

"No. Just nervous," Shredder said. "I smile when I'm nervous."

Houston turned his head and looked at Shredder like he'd lost his mind. It seemed obvious that Shredder hadn't had an opportunity to fill him in on the plan. At least Shredder looked alert and ready to act once I did my part. While the kidnapper had a gun, he hadn't tied either man up. That would work in our favor.

"Thirty-six seconds to live, gentlemen. I guess your friend isn't going to make it as I hoped she would. Any last words?"

Neither man said anything. I could feel the tension in the kidnapper's body as he prepared to squeeze the trigger, which was pointed at Houston's head.

Deciding the time was now, I said the words I'd decided on to make my presence in his mind evident for the first time.

"Sarah loved the man you used to be. She'd hate the man you've become. You know she wouldn't want you to do this."

He paused, dropping his arm just a bit. Shredder was watching for this and jumped forward. The men struggled, and the gun went off, but since Shredder was stronger and much more skilled, he was able to tackle the man to the floor. As the man hit the floor, the gun skidded across the room. Houston seemed to shake off the remainder of the effects of the sedative as he scurried across the room and grabbed the gun. Once I realized the men were safe, I started to sob uncontrollably.

Chapter 24

It had been two weeks since the longest, most intense night of my life. Actually, I supposed the night I almost lost Shredder and Houston was the second longest and most intense night of my life. The night I lost my sister, Val, would always maintain its place as numero uno in the worst night of my life category.

Once Shredder had subdued the kidnapper, Houston had found a drape cord and tied the man's ankles and wrists. Shredder borrowed my cell phone and made a call. A black chopper had shown up within sixty minutes, and Shredder and the kidnapper had been whisked away.

The whole thing happened so quickly that I hadn't even had a chance to let Shredder know that I was glad that he hadn't died. I'd hoped he'd call or stop by at some point, but so far, he hadn't. I still didn't know who the kidnapper was or what would happen to him now that he was in custody, but I did know that the unbearable loss of the love of his life was the catalyst that set off the series of events that led to the second longest night of my life.

Once Shredder had left, Houston and I returned to Anchorage to check out of our rooms and return the rental cars. We booked the first flight home we could find. Once the remainder of the sedative Houston had been given had worn off, he seemed fine. I'd asked him repeatedly if he was fine, and he said he was, but something felt different. He'd been through a traumatic experience, and I understood that he might need time to process everything, but I worried that his experience had changed something between us. Something, I fretted, that we might not be able to repair.

Jake said to give him space, so I gave him space. He went to work, and I divided my time between the animal shelter, Neverland, and my cabin. I walked my dogs, chatted with the locals who frequented the bar, and hung out with Harley once Brittany had grown bored and left. While my life settled back into normal, routine, and comfortable, I had to admit, if only to myself, that there was a gnawing in my gut that seemed to whisper that something was missing.

"Oh good, you're here," Serena greeted me when I entered the shelter. She and Harley were standing at the counter, looking at something that appeared to be a flier of some sort.

"What do you have there?" I asked.

"The flier for the annual fundraising benefit," Serena answered. "This year, Harley made use of his celebrity superpower and got us one of the hottest bands in the country."

She pointed to the name of the band, and I had to admit I was impressed. "Wow. That's really awesome. We should raise a ton of money. Enough to pay for the wild animal expansion and maybe to do some upgrades to the domestic animal side."

"That's the plan," Harley responded. He glanced at his watch. "I need to get going. I have a call with my agent in an hour." He glanced at Serena. "See you tonight?"

"I'll be ready."

With that, Harley kissed both Serena and me on the cheek and left.

"Tonight?" I asked.

"Don't get too excited. Harley and I have a business date to go over the new budget, but he is taking me to dinner, so I'm sort of counting it as a date."

"Sounds promising. Where are you going?"

"That new steakhouse on the lake."

I raised a brow. "Very nice. I think the fact that Harley chose such a nice restaurant makes a statement."

She grinned. "Do you think so?"

I shrugged. "I don't know. Like I've said many times, Harley is a nice guy. He goes the extra mile.

The fact that he's taking you to the nicest restaurant in the area for your budget meeting may or may not mean anything. Either way, I hope you have a nice time."

"Oh, I plan to. I have a killer new dress that I doubt even a famous action star will fail to notice."

I turned and smiled as Houston entered the shelter. "Hey, stranger. How are you feeling?"

"Better." He gave me a long hard hug. "Can we talk?"

"I need to get going," Serena said, making herself scarce.

I returned my attention to Houston as I felt my chest tighten. "Sure. There's no one in the training room. Let's head there."

Once we were settled onto stools that lined the walls, I asked him what was up.

"As you know, my boss has been encouraging me to take some time off after what happened. In fact, he's insisting on it. At first, I didn't want to take the time he wanted me to have, but then I realized that I really could use a break." He paused and swallowed hard. "An old buddy of mine from way back rented a house in Cancun. He asked me to join him for a couple weeks. I thought about it and decided that might be just what I need."

I forced a smile I wasn't feeling. "That sounds fun. I hope you have a wonderful time."

"I really just want some peace and quiet and time to think about things."

"I get it," I said.

"Have you heard from Shredder?"

"Not a word."

He frowned. "That's too bad. I keep hoping we'll get news about the man's identity or the fate of the woman from MI6 and the man from Interpol."

"Yeah," I agreed. "It would be nice, but that may very well be information we'll never have. I hoped I'd recognize the kidnapper once I got a look at him, but I didn't. I really have no idea who he was or how he knew I was wearing a yellow sweater, but I don't think he actually spent time inside the shelter. He must have been lurking in the parking lot."

Houston didn't respond. He seemed distracted. I could almost see the battle that must have been going on in his mind as it played out on his face.

"When are you leaving?" I asked.

"Tomorrow."

I had to admit that I hadn't been expecting that.

He reached out a hand and ran a finger down my cheek. It almost felt as if he was committing my face to memory.

"Maybe we can get together when you get back," I suggested. "I'll make you dinner."

"Sounds nice." He slipped off the stool. He hugged me one more time for a really long time, and then he turned and walked away. As he walked through the door, I couldn't help but wonder if we'd ever have that dinner or if this would turn out to be our final goodbye.

USA Today best-selling author Kathi Daley lives in beautiful Lake Tahoe with her husband, Ken. When she isn't writing, she likes spending time hiking the miles of desolate trails surrounding her home. Find out more about her books at www.kathidaley.com

Printed in Great Britain
by Amazon